SACRED KING: RICHARD I[II]

SINNER, SUFFERER, SCAPE[GOAT]

BY J.P. REEDMAN

Copyright 2014—Herne's Cave Publishing

REVISED SECOND EDITION 2015

Cover art by FRANCES QUINN

Chapter One—THE CASTLE OF CARE

A warm but strong August wind, a wind that heralded change and summer's end, swirled around the bastions of Nottingham castle, standing high on its rock with the Trent pushing sluggishly at its adamant foot. Twilight crept over the bailey; the frowning foursquare keep; the sturdy inner bridge with its array of eroded gargoyles and griffins, some dating from the reign of King John nearly three hundred years before. It had been that unfortunate and inept King's favourite castle.

It was no longer so for Richard Plantagenet, who had also once favoured Nottingham—Richard the Third, King of England, Lord of Ireland. This place, though once a happy residence, had now become his 'Castle of Care.' A place of bitter memory, a place of sorrow.

High in the great tower on the northern wall, which had been fashioned into grand apartments by Richard's brother Edward IV, then expanded and beautified further by Richard's own hand, the King sat signing documents in his chamber by the light of a single taper. He had dismissed his squires and attendants for the evening; the King wished to be alone more and more these days, these hard long days since...*since*...

Seeing the sky fade to purple with impending dusk, he glanced up towards the window. The pen in his hand sank to the table, splattering ink like traceries of shadow. Soon it would be too dark to see the words written on the paper...

He sighed and stood up stiffly, stretching his back and shoulders as best he could. It gave him great pain tonight, his spine with its twist to the right, a dull endless ache and stiffness running from his right shoulder to the small of his back, but that nagging pain could be endured; he had learned to accept it long ago. For his other pain, there was no relief and no chance of acceptance.

The pain of memory....

He leaned awkwardly in the window embrasure, gazing out into the growing gloom. The brown hair brushing his shoulders absorbed the wavering light; blue-grey eyes turned the colour of the faded sky. Shadows stretched under those too-old eyes, marks of grief dark and painful as bruises. It was only just over a year since he had been in Nottingham with Anne, and their lives had changed forever....

April 6, a date he would never forget, carved into his mind as if by a blade, never to be forgotten, a wound never to heal. Spring had come late that year, the night chill as deadly as that of December, the frost sparkling on the grass and the buds killed on the trees. The wind had roared and howled then, as it did now—as it often did on Nottingham's high rock above the bustling and ancient town with its slums, stews, churches, and taverns such as The Trip to Jerusalem and the Gabriel-Comes-unto-the-Virgin-Mary, which nestled near the foot of Castle hill.

Richard had been ready to retire for the night; the bedchamber was warm, with the fire burning hot, stoked up by the servants to keep out the endless cold that seeped through the ancient stonework. Drafts moved the hangings on the wall and curled the lavish velvet curtains that swathed the rails of the bed.

"Anne, what ails you?" Sitting on the bedside wearing just a red gown, Richard had glanced over at his wife, slightly irritated, slightly perplexed. "Come to bed, you look weary."

Anne had not been herself all evening. She had eaten little at table, picking at her food as though it curdled in her belly, and now she paced the chill floor in her nightgown like some caged beast, a woolen cloak thrown over her shoulders for added warmth. Despite the cloak, and despite the heat of the merry blaze in the brazier, she was visibly shivering and her cheeks were white as the frost on the windowsill.

He had gazed at her solemnly and wished she would cease her fretting and come to him. Anne was not an acclaimed beauty like the ice-gilt Elizabeth Woodville, wed to his brother Edward in a secret in a May Day marriage that Ned had probably truly never intended to honour, but she was beautiful in her own way, for any who had the eyes to see.

Long thick hair hung down past her hips, her most striking feature, neither brown nor blonde nor red, but a mixture of all three colours, earth and fire and sunlight. Its swirl in the warm light captivated him, made him want to run his thin fingers through its length as he had done so many times over the long years of their marriage. He had fought hard for her, against the will of his brother George...fickle dead George, drowned by Edward's decree in a vat of Malmsey and buried beside his wife Isabel in Tewkesbury...

Yes, Anne's lands were attractive to Richard, the great wealth she brought as the daughter of Warwick and Anne Beauchamp, but they were good together. *His beloved consort.*

"Anne," he said hoarsely, "you will make yourself ill, if you fret so, and you have always been frail. Come, lie down..."

"It's the wind..." She approached the window embrasure, gazing out into the night. Leaves ripped from trees swirled by on the gale. There was no light beyond the casement, no moon, not a solitary star. Blackness, dark as the grave. "I hate the sound of the wind here. I wish we were back in Middleham with Edward."

Richard got up and approached her, wrapping his own robe about her to give her added warmth. She felt so thin against his body, her ribs and hipbones sharp. Richard and Anne were small people, both of similar height and both small-framed and lean, with no excess fat on either of them, but Anne's thinness felt unhealthy, and indeed she was often ill, wracked by a cough that tore at her chest, while Richard was seldom bothered by illness...he had left such maladies behind with childhood.

"Be not grieved, sweetling, we will head north before long," he murmured into her shining hair, drawing her head to his shoulder in an attempt to settle her. She felt so cold, not just thin, but cold as if she were a woman made of stone, an effigy in a church. The thought of the tomb, unbidden, made Richard grow uneasy; it was like an omen, a foreshadowing. "I am sure the wind shrieks just as fiercely in Middleham as it does in Nottingham!"

"But it is a wind we know…at home," she whispered. Her eyes were big, feverish; the candle flames on the bedside reflected in them, making them look strange, unearthly. "This is a foreign wind, and there is something dark at its heart."

Richard felt a pang of nameless fear and crossed himself. Another blast of the wind shook the candles around the chamber. The flames bent sideways, streaming, and then guttered. Anne's eyes, lit so unnaturally, went suddenly dark. She gasped and her hands clutched at his, seeking reassurance.

An urgent knock sounded on the door. Echoes ran down the corridor like the thumping of a heart.

"Do not open it!" Anne's voice rose, sharp with fear. Her fingernails dug into Richard's hand.

"Anne, I…I must…" He prised her from his arms, threw a thick cloak over his shoulders, and opened the door, suddenly grim-faced. A night message could only bode ill—invasion, or worse.

Francis Lovell, Richard's friend from childhood, stood in the soot-streaked passage outside the King's chamber, his eyes bleak and strained in a face that held an unusual chalky pallor. A messenger stood next to him, equally ashen-hued, covered in mud from a hard ride, his hair a thicket of twigs and leaves. Behind the messenger cowered an aged priest, bald head beaded with sweat, his cheeks florid and his hands visibly trembling as he clutched his pectoral cross.

There was a dreadful pause as Richard looked at the three men and they looked at him.

Then the messenger moved, sinking gracelessly to one knee, half in collapse. "Your Grace," he gasped, his voice heavy with emotion and exhaustion. "I bring news from the north."

The first thought that hit Richard was that the Scots had attacked England, breaking signed treaties and pillaging pivotal towns like Berwick and even York. But the expression on Lovell's usually amiable face told him that something far worse had occurred, and a cold sickness rose in Richard's gut; his mouth went dry and tasted bitter iron.

Francis took a stiff step towards the King…not just his King, but also his friend for many years. "Oh God,

Dickon..." he stammered, uncaring that he used such overt familiarity in front of the others.

"Just tell me!" Ignoring Francis, Richard grabbed the shoulder of the messenger, his fingers crushing, and dragged him to his feet. "Speak, damn you!"

The man's wind-chapped lips twisted and words spewed out like bitter poison. "Your Grace, it is evil news I bring. The...the Prince of Wales. He has died at Middleham after a brief illness, and is now in God's care."

Those words. Those dreadful words. Like a physical blow...a blow harder than any that Richard had received in battle, tearing into his heart like a sword blade. He staggered back, felt Francis's hand on his arm, steadying him, once again uncaring of the inappropriate familiarity, and he saw the candle flames dip and dive and the whole chamber fade to near-black for a terrifying instant.

And then, sharp as the pain that ripped his soul to shreds, he heard Anne screaming and screaming, over and over, above that terrible wind that had brought tidings of death and despair upon its frigid breath...

It was a wind like that tonight, singing in the battlements, rattling the casements, bringing back unwanted memories. What news would it bring to him this time?

Even as he thought on the terrible events of last spring, he caught the sound of muffled voices in the hallway beyond the stout chamber door, and then heard a familiar pounding on the aged wood...so reminiscent of last spring, when his world, his hopes had crumbled. The sound had almost been expected.

But now he was ready for any news, anticipating the worst...and there was nothing could bring him more grief than what he had already endured—the death of Edward, and then, months later, of Anne, fading away from illness and grief while the court whispered that he no longer shared her bed (*the doctors had forbidden me!*) and desired to wed his own niece (*maybe I did favour Elizabeth too much, seeking to needle Henry Tudor when he prated of marrying her himself...but my true plan after God took Anne was to seek marriage with Joanna of Portugal, and so join York with the*

House of Lancaster. Elizabeth…I sought a match for her with Manuel of Beja, not with me!)

Slowly Richard opened the door. A messenger stood in the flickering torchlight, muddy and windswept as the one who had come last year, surrounded by others, his most loyal men, vague shadows in the gloom. "Your news?" Richard's voice was steady.

The man told him. Outside the wind moaned, a thing in pain.

Richard smiled a bitter weary smile that did not reach his eyes.

Lammastide, the old feast of thanksgiving, had not long gone past, and Henry Tydder's forces were on the way, sailing across the expanse of the Channel. They would make it to Britain's shores this time, unless God acted against them and brought another great storm…as He had done during Henry's last attempt at landing during Buckingham's failed rebellion.

Richard did not think that would happen again…God had seen fit to take and take from him this past year and he no longer dared to dream of aid from above. Despite the gravity of the news he had received, he felt a strange, dark gladness.

A sense of overwhelming relief.

No more waiting. No more wondering.

Soon, one way or another, there would be an end.

Chapter Two—THE WILD HUNT

King Richard rode out of the gates of Nottingham castle with his hunting party gathered around him. Bright and majestic as knights from the Courts of King Arthur, they cantered down Castle hill and through the bustling town, skirting the market square with its stalls and animal pens and passing St Mary's as they took the road to the Royal Park of Bestwood, where a hunting lodge had stood for centuries amongst the stout oaks and ash.

People gathered in the streets, skinny urchins in rags, dyers and tanners stained to the armpits, bakers ghostly with flour on their faces, goodwives in finery with their fat merchant husbands, and all manner of men who tumbled out of unsavoury inns, half-inebriated, to stare at their ruler and his companions as they passed on the way to their sport.

Rumours of Henry Tydder's forthcoming invasion had filtered down to the common folk of Nottingham and the crowd was subdued, save for the exuberant, unwitting children—their eyes were heavy and anxious, even suspicious. It did not seem normal to them that on the brink of war, the King rode out to hunt as if no danger threatened the land.

"He does not look afraid..." a crone whispered as she sat on a stool outside the cookshop where she hawked meat pies with her friend, Margerie. The old woman itched the ripening wen on her nose and stared critically at the retreating figure of the King on his fine horse. "But, bless him, he looks so thin and white; he needs a good meal and a good robust bedmate who'll give him an heir. No disrespect intended to late Queen Anne, God rest her soul."

"Why would King Richard look afraid, Peg?" asked her rotund companion, Margerie, wiping sweat from the mottled platter of her face with her sleeve. Last night's storm had blown out the rain and ushered in hot, sticky, thunderous weather. "When has he ever lost a battle? As for that Henry

Tydder, he's untried in the field and has only his foreign sorts to support 'im for the most part."

"It's a foolish man who ain't afraid of war, Margerie. Even a King. And they say God don't smile on him 'cos of how 'e got the crown. Look at his poor wee mite the Prince of Wales. Dead. And Queen Anne, dead too, on a day when the sun went dark and day turned to night…Some said he had 'er poisoned so he could take a new wife…but that ain't true; it hasn't happened."

"Don't speak of it, Peg." The bigger woman peered at the cloudless summer sky as if she expected the sun to suddenly fall from it, just as it had on the day the poor Queen died. "That could be seen as treasonous talk."

Peg sniffed, scratched at her ripe wen again. "I'll wager there's greater treason than that brewin', Margerie. Mark my words. Mark my words, girl. Treason."

Bestwood was part of the great forest of Sherwood, famed in legend as a haunt of outlaws and of darker things, of spirits that dwelt in the trees and in the earth and in deep woodland pools rumoured to be bottomless. On the east and west, two great roads formed the boundaries of the Royal Park, one wending its way to Mansfield and the other, the King's Highway, running all the way to York. Ancient native woodland clashed with plantations of fruit-bearing trees, shadowing the darting deer that ran free through Appletree Dale, Holyndale, Elder Tree Dale and over King's Oak Hill.

Richard led the hunting party down the winding stretch of Rederode, the Red Road, on the edge of the Park. At its farthest end, Bestwood's edge was marked by a spring and a stream that fed into the River Leen. At some point in time, this water had been dammed to form a pool, and another stream, the Holy Stone Seke, continued a meandering path through the birch, alder, and willow that loved marshy places. This area was a choice place to find quarry, for animals frequently emerged from the heavy foliage to drink from the water.

As the King's party approached the shores of the pool, the lean greyhounds and vicious alaunts who sometimes even bit their own masters, lifted their heads and began to whine and bark with excitement.

"They sense something," muttered Richard Ratcliffe, as one hound leaped forward, snapping, to be brought back to heel with a sharp command. "I have never seen the dogs so agitated before."

King Richard peered into the shadows across the pond, its waters dark and strangely still, unruffled by the wind. Sun glimmered upon its surface but did not seem to penetrate its depth; the only motion was of long green weeds, tossing like submerged hair in the darkness below. It unnerved him, and he made to glance away…and in the corner of his vision, caught sight of a moving shape between the trees, the reflection of white legs, white flanks breaking the mirror-like surface on the water's edge.

He had not expected to see such blinding whiteness.

Nor did he expect to see a huge Hart, much larger than any he had hunted before, crash through the weeping willows on the farthest bank, and stand stone-still on the bank, its head turned in his direction as if it gazed straight at him. Ghostly-pale, its antlers scored the sky like daggers, many-tined and fierce, with vines and mosses twined around them and flapping as it tossed its head.

What a magnificent animal and, in its pure whiteness, so rare! Richard breathed a long, awe-filled sigh, his eyes drinking in the sight. The Hart was deemed a holy beast; some even compared it to Christ for its suffering at the hands of man. St Eustace's conversion from paganism had been instigated by seeing such a majestic animal with a crucifix shining between its antlers.

The white Hart seemed to observe Richard with eyes full of knowledge and a power that was almost human. It tossed its antlers as if gesturing him to seek pursuit, and then, with a snort of mist from flared nostrils, its thigh muscles bunched and it sprang away into the gloom of the forest.

A challenge! The dogs went wild, yammering and baying...but, oddly, they slunk around the startled riders as if fearing to spring forward.

Richard felt his heart leap. It was the first time he had felt truly alive for days...no, months...ever since he had buried Anne in Westminster Abbey. Without even a glance at the rest of the hunting party, he drove his heels into his horse's flanks and galloped in pursuit of the great white Hart.

Behind him, he heard faint shouts, the voices full of alarm, amidst the wild gabble of the baying dogs. He paid no heed. A mist was rising, born out of the heat of the day mixed with the coolness of the water and the damp ground. It closed in on him like a vice, cutting him off from his men, from the dogs, from the well-known paths of the forest.

He was riding blind through Bestwood, under strange trees that dipped and swayed as if they had suddenly come alive, possessed of some primal forest spirit. His horse seemed terrified; he could feel its flanks trembling beneath the pressure of his knees. It snorted and shied away from shrub and gnarled oak; dancing hooves hit mushrooms that exploded in a puff of spores.

A lesser horseman might have feared being thrown from the saddle but not Richard Plantagenet. He had ridden all his life, crossing the wild moors and rushing ghylls of Yorkshire on many occasions, even in inclement weather—gales, heavy snow, lashing rain. When he was on horseback, he felt truly part of the beast, its body an extension of his, its power harnessed for his use. He was a small man next to some of the brawny giants in his retinue, but when he was mounted, he not only equalled them, but often surpassed them in strength and agility.

His quarry this day would not escape him. By God, he would track the mysterious Hart down, and bring it back to Nottingham as a token of his victory over it. A victory soon to be replicated when he took the field against Henry Tydder....

Ahead the mist began to lift slightly; he could see the waters of the lake lying to his left. Dull slate grey, it shone with a strange light that seemed to radiate from under the surface rather than from the sun. A little tongue of land jutted into the waters; a single mighty oak grew upon it, flanked by ancient yews, the tree of the graveyard and of archers.

For an instant, he thought he spied the white Hart, prancing under the boughs where the leaves showed just the first hint of Autumn's decline, but when he blinked his eyes, the beast was gone. There was no sign of the Hart at all, but in its place were two unfamiliar men, one kneeling in the mud, while the other hovered behind him. Both seemed unaware of the King's presence.

Poachers? Richard drew rein and frowned into the murk. His elation at the chase faded and a chill went through him. Sudden, sickly fear knotted under his breastbone, reminding him of the awful days in the summer of 1483 when he had been unable to eat, sleep or drink, and he was sure he had been ill-wished by the Woodville witch Elizabeth Grey, who was daughter of Jacquetta of Bedford, noted witch and descendent of the river-spirit Melusine. The taint of the unholy hung about these unknown men; a hint of strangeness, of something dark and old, primeval. Something he did not understand, and did not wish to understand.

No, no, he shook his head to deny his fears; these were but lowly poachers surely, for all that they were dressed outlandishly, like mummers or characters in a Mystery Play.

The one kneeling in the mud wore but a tanned hide, like a savage, a woodwose who ran wild in the forest. Bare knees poked out from beneath the primitive covering. Shaggy dark hair, rudely trimmed, framed a bearded face of strength and character; but he was ghost-pale and looked dazed, as if drugged or drunk. He held up his arms to the sky and Richard spotted a strange band circling his bicep; a bracelet of plaited fox fur.

The man behind him was older, a Merlin figure out of Geoffrey of Monmouth's *Historia Regum Britanniae*, with silverish hair streaming like a cloud around him and his face, cracked like the bottom of a dry river, stern and adamant. On his head, he wore the most extraordinary headgear—a cap made from the skull-pate of a deer with gnarly antlers sprouting from it. The tall horns, silhouetted against the sky, were what made Richard initially mistake him for the Hart he hunted.

Richard crossed himself; the sight of this ancient man in his long robe fringed with animal teeth made him uneasy. He thought of the legend from the time of Richard II, of Herne the Hunter with his ragged antlers, a suicide whose spirit haunted the forests around Windsor and rode with a Wild Hunt from Hell...

The old man made a jerky movement; in his hand appeared a stone axe bound to a haft of polished wood. Richard had seen such implements before; farmers sometimes turned them up in their fields, especially if they ploughed to close to old, long mounds where human bones were wont to lie. They were curiosities but not to be kept; some thought they were the leavings of fairies, or devils; though others thought they conferred protection against thunder and buried them under their doorsteps. Whatever they were, they were not wholesome, not fitting tools for Christian men to touch or admire...

The antlered man raised the axe and brandished it at the strange sky; Richard's unwilling gaze stole to the polished stone axe-head, crude but heavy, tapering to a point at one end. It descended like a thunderclap, and struck the back of the skull of the kneeling man, a blow as fatal as that of a modern-day sword or halberd.

The man slumped forward, and his attacker, finishing the act, drew a knife of bronze and slit his throat, before thrusting the bleeding corpse into the marshy shallows of the lake, where it began to sink amidst the leaves and reeds.

Another cold chill ran through Richard, almost as if, as superstitious goodwives would say, some creature had bounded over his unknown grave. He almost felt the impact of the stone axe, a shuddering blow, and a wave of dizziness nearly cast him from his horse's back—he who was normally an expert horseman, at one with his mount as if they were a single being.

Shaking his head to clear it, he quickly recovered his equilibrium. He drew his sword, a flash amidst the rising mist. He had witnessed a murder here, in the King's forest, *his* forest, and he could not brook such an affront. Whoever this man was, he would bring him to justice, and if...if he were not a true man but some devil, by Christ, he would deal with him too! Resolve hardening, he spurred his pawing, reluctant mount toward the antlered man.

The mist rolled in again, descending like a cap, making trees into lurching monsters and dulling all sound. It smelt foul, dead; Richard cursed and then crossed himself again. This was surely unnatural, Satan's work. The Devil was always seeking to confound and torment mortal men, and he, a sinner of the worst sort, bearing the guilt that all kings carried, especially those who reigned in times of strife, was a likely candidate for torment by the Prince of Darkness. And if not devils...then this was surely magecraft wrought by sorcerers, conjurors and alchemists like George Ripley, who had dedicated his works to Richard's brother King Edward. Richard's elder brother had been much intrigued with such arts, much to Richard's disgust.

The King glanced around him; he could see nothing in the swirling sheet of grey, neither the antlered man, nor the corpse of his victim. Suddenly a wet droplet struck his cheek, ran like a tear; he wiped it with his gloved hand and inhaled noisily in shock as he saw his fingers were red.

Glancing upwards, to his horror he saw a man hanging from the gaunt tree branches above, twirling slowly from a noose made of hemp rope.

The hanged man's head hung at a crooked angle, his face blue; bloody droplets spilled from the yawning mouth. He resembled the man in the antlered headdress but his garb was less primitive though still coarse and gaudily dyed, like that of a figure from an old story. He had only one eye, one orbit was a gaping hollow, the other filled with a milky blue, dead eye that stared into otherness.

How could the stranger have got up there to take his life so fast? And where had the other men gone, both slayer and slain? Richard was perplexed. He debated whether he should cut the man down and give him some dignity in death, but decided that he would leave the body for the foresters; the stranger was a trespasser, after all, and maybe associated with the killing he had witnessed on the lakeshore.

The body on its rope was swinging slightly faster now, round and round, then back and forth, as if caught in a strong wind, though Richard could feel no fresh breeze upon his upturned face. His horse began to struggle for control of the bit again, and to shudder—long chills that Richard could feel against his thighs.

Abruptly the corpse stopped moving, hanging in the boughs like a long shadow. Its mouth gaped, then, horribly, the corpse in the tree began to speak. *"Nine nights I hung on the sacred tree, a sacrifice of myself to myself.'*

Richard crossed himself again and drew his sword, forcing his hand not to shake. He had fearlessly joined in many a battle but never against any being that did not seem of the world of men. By the Blood of Christ, he would not brook this kind of foulness in his forest, and he would smite this foul being to a second death and drive it into the Hell it deserved.

The dangling body stared down, milky single eye shining with silver fire and its lips writhing like blue snakes around teeth sharp as daggers. Again, the Hanged Man spoke, cryptic words once more, but this time they seemed more directed to the King:

Cattle die and kinsmen die,
thyself too soon must die,
but one thing never, I ween, will die,
fair fame of one who has earned.
Cattle die and kinsmen die,
thyself too soon must die,
but one thing never, I ween, will die,
the doom on each one dead.

A flame of anger kindled in Richard's breast as he heard the prophetic words, full of dire warning. "Do you know to whom you speak?" he cried. "Do you know it is treason to ill-wish the King?"

The cold, white face craned toward him, its one glazed blue eye starting horribly from its socket with the pressure of the noose round the throat. "No man may live whom the fates doom at dawning…" Its breath flowed forth as a vile mist, like that which had risen so suddenly in Bestwood.

Richard's patience snapped, driven by the fear of enchantment, of sorcery, of Satan's work. He swung at the figure with his blade…and at the same time, the sorcerous mist rolled in again, wafting in great gouts from the Hanged Man's jaws and swirling around the forest like a grey, ragged shroud encompassing a corpse.

The King glanced wildly around, fearing an assault from behind and feeling all too vulnerable in his unarmoured and disorientated state, but then he heard the yelling of hounds and the shouts of familiar voices, and as he turned his horse's head toward the welcome noise, the mist-cloak ripped apart and the sun glimmered amidst the trees of Bestwood, welling through the veins of leaves tinted with the first hint of Autumn's gold.

Glancing over his shoulder, he saw the tree where the man—the prophet, the demon—had hung, but the figure was gone, the branches empty of their foul fruit. The tree, an oak, was dead and its boughs, raking the sky, were like the gnarly antlers of an old stag. A large crow perched on a branch cawing loudly, mockingly, its head cocked to one side. Richard stared at it, and it stared back at him impudently; it seemed to have only one eye…

Now, Richard Ratcliffe rode up, breathless and windblown. "Your Grace, thank heavens you are here! We were worried when you outstripped us by so far. We searched for you, but it was as if you vanished from the face of the earth."

"The stag…the white stag…I wanted to bring it down. I thought you were all behind me."

Ratcliffe stared, perplexed. "Your Grace? A stag?"

"Did you not see it? No? Maybe that accursed mist off the lake hid it too well."

Ratcliffe shook his head uneasily. "Your Grace, we saw no beast and no mist either. Just your person riding away with all speed…and then we could see you no more. But that must be a minor thing, a trick of the light. We are educated men and do not believe in the old forest spirits as did our ancestors.

However, while you rode without us, word has come of other evil devils, ones of mortal flesh and bone."

Dick Ratcliffe's face turned solemn, his lips compressed lines. "As we searched for you, my liege, a messenger arrived at the Lodge. Word has come at last from the Lord Lovell and others. Henry Tudor has not landed on the south coast as predicted but at Milford Haven. He is on the march with his army of brigands, traitors and mercenaries, and seeks to bolster his numbers by appealing to the dubious loyalties of the Welsh."

Richard's eyes glittered; this was the news he had been waiting for. The strangeness of his last hour faded from his mind, as matters of greater import took over. Maybe his grim vision was from too much sun, or too little sleep (he oftentimes slept poor) or was even indeed a trick of some malicious unseen force, seeking to unman him.

No matter. It was not time to ponder unwholesome imaginings, but a time to act decisively, for the sake of the kingdom. "We knew this day would come soon. Let us go forth and meet him. You say he seeks alliance with the Welsh? What of Ap Thomas? He swore an oath that if Tudor reached Wales, he would have to pass over his body before he could come any further."

Dick Ratcliffe stared down at his boots; he did not wish to tell Richard the truth, fearing a burst of royal Plantagenet rage, but there was no other choice. The King had to be told. "Ap Thomas has turned your Grace, curse his disloyalty. He got round his vows to you by lying 'neath a bridge while Tudor and his men rode over it!"

Richard stared at Ratcliffe, eyes widening with rage at the news. But he kept control; some defections must be expected—many men were partial to bribes, and some of the Welsh regarded Tydder as one of their own.

"It matters not," he said curtly, "he will not get past my son-in-law Herbert at any rate, so the points where he can access England will be limited; perhaps through Ludlow or Shrewsbury. Send more spies and watchers to the West so that we know exactly in what direction he marches. I will gather my army in all haste and ride towards Leicester. I expect Tydder will try and turn towards London, and he must be stopped before he gets there."

Excitement rose in Richard as he gave his orders. Yes, the time was here, to throw off the dark shackles of doubt that had constrained him since he took the throne. The rebellions, the rumours of murder. He would defeat his rival and then marry Joanna of Portugal. Her portrait did not promise beauty, but it was said she was pious and intelligent, and that mattered more to him that a comely face. She was not young, which counted against her in regards to producing an heir, but he knew he was a fertile man. Though poor Anne had only given him his lost Ned, he had two natural children, John and Katherine, and there was no reason why he should not beget more... Look at his brother Edward, ten children with the Woodville bitch and a pack of other bastards...

He turned his thoughts from unwelcome musings on his elder brother's children. The two lords bastard, Edward and Richard, in the Tower. Bastards that had been princes until Bishop Stillington, old and tremulous, had delivered his tale of Edward's contracted marriage with Eleanor Butler. Locked away for their safety. They had played on the lawn, many had seen them shooting at butts. Then there had been the plot to free them. They had to be moved; the Duke of Buckingham had insisted on it.

And then....

Richard shuddered and the warmth fled from the afternoon. A shadow smeared the lake and he remembered once again what he had seen in the forest—the murder and the corpse in the water, its skull riven; the Hanged Man with his all-seeing dead eye....

But there was no time to mull over the witchery of this primeval woodland on the border of Sherwood. He had to deal with the here and now.

And with Henry Tydder, his mortal enemy, who was now on the march.

Chapter Three: NIGHT AT THE BLUE BOAR

The army of King Richard marched toward Leicester beneath the burning August sun. Richard rode bareheaded before the host, while peasants in the fields paused in their toil to watch the spectacle of their King heading off to war. Children ran at the roadside and fat women with dirty faces and babes bundled in their arms jostled for the best position to view the soldiers and knights as they headed toward their destination. Dust and noise ascended to heaven, horse harness jingled and bright banners snapped in the wind. Baggage trains groaned beneath their burdens of weapons and provisions.

Resounding cheers rose in waves; Richard could hear the noise as he rode by upon White Syrie, but a note of unease marred the raised voices, a shadow of doubt thinned them. The common folk waxed fearful, and who could blame them? None could predict how the Wheel of Fortune would turn, and a promised fair harvest could easily become burnt earth and death. Indeed, rumours had reached his ears that Tydder's rag-tag army of rogues and thieves, the detritus of France's prisons, had trampled crops with impunity upon approaching the fields around Atherstone, laughing at the distress of the villagers. Before setting out, Richard had forbidden such behaviors among his own men, with strong penalties promised if word came of any such misdeeds.

Up ahead, Richard saw through the heat-haze the great bastion of Leicester's North Gate, its portcullis raised and gleaming, the tips of the spikes like a row of dragon's teeth. Shadows stretched over him, and he felt a flush of coolness after the day's heat as he passed below the arch. He was glad to be here after the hasty march from Nottingham, even if tomorrow he would have to move on again to confront Henry Tydder.

Passing beneath the massive, turreted gateway, the King rode sedately up a packed High Street, until he reached the inn known as 'The Blue Boar', a seemly place to stay for the night before resuming the road to conflict. It was a handsome tavern, timber-framed and neatly kept, with painted shutters and angels and mythic beings carved on the gables.

Richard was used to staying in such wayside inns; if he had ruled a hundred years earlier, he would have stayed in Leicester castle, its bailey hard by the river Soar, but when he had visited it two years ago, he found it growing ruinous, cracks snaking through the stonework, its chambers damp and almost uninhabitable. The castle's Great Hall was as undamaged. however, and still appropriate for meetings, while for prayer he fancied nearby St Mary de Castro, where his father, Richard of York, had been knighted as a youth, but he would not sleep in such a dank, unwelcoming place as Leicester castle until peace came and he had the time to order repairs to the dilapidation.

Drawing reign outside the Blue Boar Inn, Richard dismounted White Syrie, handing the reins to a sweaty-faced, nervous ostler, who led the stallion to the stables at the rear of the building. Chaos ensued as a barrage of servants ran hither and thither in the inn's cobbled courtyard; trunks and chests were lugged up the steep stairs, and food and drink arrived in a never-ending stream of carts.

Richard could see the innkeeper lurking in the doorframe, rubbing his thick read hands and beaming at the honour of providing a room to the King. Beside him flounced his good-wife, a buxom dame in a yellow cap, and three young maids Richard presumed were the man's daughters, all wearing freshly laundered dresses and trying to coyly catch a glimpse of the King.

He smiled wryly to himself. No doubt, they wanted to see if he in any wise resembled tall, god-like Edward, who in youth had been called the Rose of Rouen due to possessing such exceptional beauty. Alas, the maidens would surely find him lacking, with his pale serious face, thin limbs and lack of height. But no matter…unlike his brother, 'the Rose', he had not much interest in the charms and delights of passing tavern wenches.

The King turned to one of his attendants, who had reached Leicester ahead of the Royal Army to prepare for his arrival. "Has my bed arrived in the train?"

The man bowed to the ground. "Yes, your Grace."

Richard entered the Blue Boar, as people bowed and curtseyed all around him, bobbing up and down like logs on a river. Ascending the stairs, he entered his temporary quarters—the finest, most spacious room in the inn, which had been adorned with his own tapestries and other finery to give it a welcoming and regal feel. The mullioned window was thrown open, due to the August heat; he could see in the distance one of Leicester's many churches, St Nicholas, with its Roman stonework, and beyond its bulk the huge arches of a Roman wall, red and warm in the late afternoon light.

He thought of the Romans who had founded the town many years ago; he admired that stalwart race, as had his father the Duke of York, whom Richard resembled in many ways, including his slight appearance, so different to that of Edward, a veritable giant of a man. Both Richard and the Duke had borne an interest in the Roman general Stilicho, who had died in battle on August 22, the anniversary of his death falling just two days away, the very day Richard proposed to confront Henry Tudor…

Richard suddenly shivered, despite the heat of the day. He hoped he was not sickening at such a crucial time. He had heard via his messengers that the Sweating Sickness was rampant in the land, probably brought by Tydder's filthy mercenaries. Thomas Stanley himself had cried off from meeting him, supposedly struck down, though recovering. If it was true (and Richard suspected it was not—Stanley was Tydder's step-father through his marriage to the Beaufort woman, Margaret) Stanley was lucky—often a man would die within the day from such a malady.

Tetchily, the King gestured for wine to soothe the dryness of his throat after the long march; attentive hands swiftly brought a golden goblet to him and he raised it to his lips. His gaze fixed on the servants as they wrestled with the panels, mattress, bolster and velvet hangings of his bed. He had brought that bed from Nottingham…indeed, he took it with him everywhere he could, stored in the baggage train. He slept ill in strange beds, for many caused his curved back to knot in pain and made him stiff as an old man the next day. He could not afford to be in anything other than perfect condition for the battle for the Crown of England.

Soon the room was ready, but rest had to wait, although Richard wished for nothing more that to stretch out on that newly assembled bed for a few hours. It was time for Vespers, and it was his wish to hear Mass in the church of St Mary Castro, up near the Great Hall of the castle. Tired as he was from the heat and the ride, the safety of a man's soul took precedence over bodily weakness. Motioning for Catesby and Ratcliffe, Brackenbury and John Kendall, and his other Knights of the Body to escort him from the room, the King left the Blue Boar Inn and passed through still-buzzing crowds towards the hilltop church, which stood connected to the Castle's Great Hall by a recently built timber-framed gateway.

As they approached the stout gate, Richard let his gaze travel up the tall, thin spire of St Mary's, darning heaven like a needle and casting a long shadow over the approaching party. Along the church's roofline gargoyles grimaced and leered, watching the King with stony eyes as he entered the porch with his entourage.

Once inside, Richard walked slowly down the long, narrow nave, lined by round Norman arches with reeded capitals, and took the seat prepared for him before the altar. Ancient skilful carvings, sedilia and the little, worn image of a page loomed out of the incense-laden gloom. The Rood Screen soared before his eyes, forming a gallery where on occasion the Gospel would be sung…but not today. His head felt unnaturally heavy, muzzy, and once again, fear of illness clawed at his belly.

Light was shining through the stained glass windows of the church, making his eyes dazzled; before the high altar the priest was intoning, "*Deus, in adiutorium meum intende. Domine, ad adiuvandum me festina. Gloria Patri, et Filio, et SpirituiSancto…*"

With a start, he saw a face form in the dust motes dancing before his eyes, long, sad, sheep-like in its simplicity. Pale, a small, pursed mouth, mournful dead eyes…Henry VI, the mad Lancastrian king.

Richard had not thought about the deposed ruler for a long time, not since he had moved the old king's bones to Windsor after men had made him something of a saint at his first tomb.

Henry, he remembered, had been knighted as a tiny child here in Mary Castro, at the same time as Richard's own father—that must be why the old King returned to trouble his thoughts. Henry, a saintly old fool plagued by bouts of insanity; so out of touch with waking life that he had cried out at the birth of his son, '*This child must have been conceived by the Holy Ghost!*'—surely a blasphemy! (Even worse, men whispered that Somerset had fathered Edward of Lancaster on Margaret of Anjou, making the crazed King a cuckold.) Still, madness was no reason for a man to be put to death, and there had been no glory in Henry's end, as there was on the battlefield...

Richard's lips tightened. Yet it had to be so. Edward's orders. Richard, as High Constable of England, supplying the means. It was for the honour of his House... everything had been for the preservation of the House of York, that so many had died for, that his father and brother Edmund had died for at Wakefield, their heads displayed afterwards on Micklegate in York. Queen Margaret had even ordered a paper crown set on the Duke's head to shame him even in death.

The King closed his eyes, dispelling those disquieting images of the past, and returned to concentrating on his prayers; prayers that he would overcome his enemies and be forgiven past trespasses against man and God. But could such absolution ever be his? Men talked, whispers spread like a canker, and he knew he had little support in the south and even less in the west—he had learned a hard lesson on that score from the rebellion of the Duke of Buckingham.

Soon Mass was over. Richard returned to the Blue Boar Inn with his party. Inside his now-immaculate chamber near the top of the Inn, he called for a bath to be drawn. Servants ran about madly under the instructions of the bathman who was in charge of the royal bath-tub, filling a huge wooden tub with pails of heated water and setting up screens around it. Feet thundered on the stairs as they rushed up and down, up and down, the bathman barking orders.

"Jesu, Catesby," Richard muttered to the lawyer, William Catesby, as he poured himself some wine and then gestured that Catesby might do likewise. "It is a hot and uncomfortable night, not the best for restfulness of mind or body."

"And there are caitiffs brawling in the street, Your Grace." Brackenbury, also in attendance in the King's bed-chamber, peered out the window and gestured towards some young men, deep in their cups, who were quarrelling over some triviality in the gutter below. "What a noise they make, doubtless over a worthless bawd! Shall I send out men have them driven away?"

Richard shrugged. "They will pass on when one has smacked the other's head or more drink calls, no doubt—they are just young fools, as we all were once, I dare say. Here, help me disrobe, and then leave me. I will bathe alone. If I need any of you again, I shall summon you."

"Are you sure, your Grace?" Brackenbury said. "If you wish we can stay and play cards or chess...or I could find a musician to give you entertainment."

Richard smiled wryly. "Not tonight, I am bone-weary. I may read awhile. Or pray." The squires helped the king to undress, laying out his robe beside the tub for when he was done. It was unusual to wash one's self when one was King, but as it was his wish, his servants were in no place to gainsay him. With a motion of his hand, he dismissed all within the chamber and they left without protest; he knew his closest knights would linger outside the door, ready to defend him if anything untoward should occur between now and the dawn.

Carefully he eased himself into the cooling water, letting it rise up around him. Like his brother Edward, he paid a barber weekly to come and wash his hair, but after the dust and sweat of the long ride, he dunked his head under, came up with water streaming in his eyes. He leaned back against the wet wooden slats, enjoying the peaceful moment, when for brief seconds he could empty his mind of all troubling thoughts. His hands, fine and graceful, drifted to lie against his ribcage. He had grown thinner since Anne and Edward's deaths; sometimes he forgot to eat, and sometimes it seemed a nervous intensity burned within him, making him restless and ill at ease. He slept poorly most nights.

He was tired now; he was not the young man he once was, burning with impatience and always on the move, despite the pain of his back. Against his will, his eyelids drifted shut. The noise of Leicester's streets and the hubbub from lower levels of the Blue Boar became a distant buzz, fading away....

He woke with a start, in the surreal incoherence between sleep and wakefulness, not quite sure of his whereabouts. Glancing down, a horrified gasp tore from his lips; he seemed to be lying in a bath full of blood, the water rising red around him. He half sprang up, as water showered over the sides of the tub...and then he uttered a bitter laugh at his own morbid fantasy.

It was sunset, a hot crimson August sunset, and outside the window the sky was bleeding red as the sun's disc descended into the west. Rays streaked across the firmament of heaven, igniting a smattering of clouds, and church towers and spires stuck out like black fingers against the failing brightness.

The reflection of the reddened sky was what he had seen in the water, nothing more, surely nothing more. Yet there had been so much blood....

Climbing unsteadily out of the wooden tub, he wrapped the thick robe that laid reverently out for him about his spare frame. He could have called for his squires to attend to him, to rub him dry and dress him, to bring entertainment, and sweetmeats, and wine, and whatever else he might desire, but tonight he truly wanted to see no one. He might have felt differently if Francis had been there, his oldest friend, but Lovell was still on the road from Southampton, hastening towards Leicester after gathering news of Tydder's arrival and advancement. He prayed Frank would reach him before the upcoming battle, but the roads were so treacherous...and men even more so.

Lying down on the great bed with its carved panels and ornate draperies, he pulled the broidered coverlet over himself and sought the sleep that came so seldom to him these days. He tossed and turned, uncomfortable, sweat trickling between his shoulder blades, half in the world of dream and half in reality, but reality was drifting away, as he fell not into peaceful slumber, but the realm of nightmare, of dark rememberings…

Faces from the past, gone now, spun through his mind like dust on the wind. Anne, coughing blood; his brother the King, fat, bloated and dead while Woodvilles circled him like waiting crows; mad, tormented George, drowned in Malmsey on Edward's orders…an ironic end to one whose tongue was loose while in his cups. Then there was Will Hastings, once a comrade in arms, Anthony Woodville spouting mournful poetry, and silver-tongued, ebullient Harry Stafford, who Richard had loved like a brother until his betrayal and rebellion. The last three men had all died on his orders; deserving of their deaths or not, they haunted him. Worse still, he saw his brother's sons, mere boys who he had set aside because there was no other way; betraying the brother he had loved…and yet surely doing God's will… bastard slips shall not take root!

But saddest of all, in his tortured dreams he saw young Ned, his own little son, frail since birth, who had died so suddenly while he was at Nottingham. He recalled the small, still form laid out in the chapel at Middleham, white candles burning at feet and head, white roses scattered around him, and how he had touched and kissed that cold brow and wept until he felt empty as if his heart had been ripped from his chest, and he could neither speak nor give comfort to Anne who needed him in her own agony ….

Richard awoke and sat up, gasping, hurling off the coverlet and reaching for the dagger that he kept close by the bedside. The room idled in darkness; the inn lay silent save for creaking timbers and the soft scurry of mice in the walls. The moon was out, a hook-like crescent framed in the window, its silver path streaming in across the floorboards.

Just dreams. Disturbing dreams… that was all. But why so many more dreams now? Richard had never slept well, and even less so when he became king, pain and worry keeping him from the rest he craved. These nightmares were different, however, these ghosts from a troubled past. He shivered, wondering what such visions might betoken.

He did not sleep again for the rest of the night.

Francis Lovell arrived the next morning, disheveled and dusty after a long hard ride from the south coast. He had killed two horses under him while on his journey, but reached the gates of Leicester shortly after dawn and had been admitted into the town by the night-watch. Seeking out the Blue Boar Inn, he gave his weary mount into the keeping of the ostlers and entered the common room, a tall figure with a weary face and clothes brown with dust.

He had expected the innkeeper's servants to escort him to a chamber where he might rest until the King was awake and ready to see him, but almost immediately, he was summoned and guided to Richard's chamber. He found Richard fully awake, wrapped in a long dark blue silk robe and sitting in a chair while breaking his fast with sops—freshly baked bread soaked in wine.

"Francis, you are here!" the King said joyfully at the sight of his oldest friend, who he had known since boyhood at Middleham Castle. He rose and embraced Lovell, kissing him on either cheek. "Come, sit with me." He gestured Francis to a chair and dismissed the rest of his servants and pages, desiring private talk.

Once the door was firmly shut, the two men drifted into the easy friendship they had always had. Francis was always mindful that Richard was his King, but away from the sight of others, behind closed doors, they could assume the demeanor of long-vanished youth and talk without overt formality. Richard took a mouthful of wine and then pushed the ewer towards Lovell, along with a slab of remaining bread. "Eat, you look weary."

"You look tired yourself, your Grace…Dickon."

"Do I? Mayhap I do. I do not sleep well these nights…." Richard passed a hand over his face; he was white, no colour in his cheeks, and dark circles ringed his eyes.

Francis tried to affect an air of confidence. "Your afflictions will be over soon, Dickon. The upstart Tudor will be dealt with, and you can rest every night thereafter."

"It is not Henry Tydder than worries me, Frank," said Richard obliquely, glancing away from his companion and staring out the window.

Francis swallowed and said nothing. He knew many things lay heavy on Richard's slight shoulders, and there were many questions he wanted to ask but dared not. There were secrets Richard felt he could not share with anyone, and Lovell knew it.

Richard smiled at his friend, though his smile was faint, the vaguest upturn of the edges of his mouth. "Come, tell me of your journeys in the south. I am glad you are here. I would not wish to be without you in the coming strife."

Francis leaned forward, reaching for the wine. "We waited for days, listening for word of Tydder's approach by sea. But he must have had word that the English ports were closed to him; the wily bastard sailed to Milford Haven and landed there."

Richard leaned back, hands folded before him; he twisted the rings on his long, thin fingers. "I had hoped the Welsh might rise up and attack him, but Rhys Ap Thomas has betrayed us. Herbert, husband to my daughter Katherine, stood firm against him at Raglan...but Herbert has not come to aid me here. I could have used his men." He sighed, shifting nervously. "A summons had been sent to York, but there is Plague in the city, and I know not what men they can spare or when the levies might arrive. Ill news...added to which, I do not trust the Stanleys, and I doubt Percy as well. William Stanley...he had already shown his true colours; my spies tell me he has met with Tudor already, and I have declared him traitor."

Francis grimaced; he had always suspected the Stanleys, as did anyone with half a brain. William Stanley was an ardent Yorkist but loyal only to Edward and to his brood—he saw Elizabeth of York as rightful heir, with her brothers missing, and was willing to accept Tudor as long as Elizabeth was Queen. Lord Stanley, on the other hand, was a notorious turncoat who would sometimes play a game in battle, where he would be on one side, his brother on the other...so one Stanley could plead for the other, since one would always been on the winning side. Of course, Thomas Stanley was stepfather to Henry Tudor himself, having married the pretender's wizened mother. Francis had never liked or trusted Henry Percy either. Percy, puffed with pride, in his great castle at Alnwick, who resented Richard's successes in the North, *his* family's traditional domain. If both Stanley and Percy were to turn on Richard…

Francis suppressed a shudder and attempted to be positive. "Still, even without Herbert's men or levies from York, our numbers still surpass Henry's," he said, deliberately not mentioning the possibility of inaction or treachery by Stanley and Percy. "We will prevail. The House of York will triumph over this untried bastard scion of a house bereft of lordship!"

"Yes…yes…you are right, it will be so!" Richard rose from his chair. Outside the sky was flushed with dawn; its red light gave added colour and life to his drained cheeks. "It is time to make ready and ride from Leicester. It is time to put this presumptuous bastard son of a tainted line in his place! We will meet him and slay him upon the Plain of Redemore."

The sun was high in the sky, shining down with all the fury of late August, when King Richard and his army left the town of Leicester, ancient Ratae on the Soar, the legendary fortress of the old British King Leir. As Richard, mounted high upon the back of White Syrie, rode down the narrow, cobbled streets between the timber-framed houses, the frenzied mobs of yesterday emerged once again, clogging the narrow streets and winding alleys.

Once more, the air grew heavy with a sense of mingled excitement and dread, and a strange festival atmosphere took over, despite the knowledge of the upcoming clash that would change all their destinies. People of all ages and stations in life thronged the streets—merchants and tradesmen, beggars and cutpurses, Grey Friars and Black Friars, women in tall henins and velvet skirts jostling raddled-faced hags in sackcloth, plump children in silks who teased urchins in rags, cordwainers and barrel-makers, dyers and tanners, fishmongers with pungent catch from the river, scowling-faced rat-catchers and the gong-farmers who shoveled shit into the gutters. The cook-shops were open and a greasy smell hung heavy in the air, worsened by the sullen heat. Piemen flogged their wares on the street corners, heavily spiced pies and sweet pastries, while other tradesmen sold hot sheep's feet and beef ribs, along with drink and seasonal fruits.

Ahead Richard could see West Gate, its towers blocking the light, and beyond its bastions the turgid river, glinting in the blaze of sunshine. Along the Soar's banks, more crowds gathered, traipsing through the mud, right up to the stalwart walls of the Austin friary that stood upon the shore on the town-side.

Riding under West Gate's arch and out over West Bridge, Richard then began the crossing of the old Bow Bridge, whose grey arches spanned the sluggish Soar. As he rode over the midsection of the bridge, a withered old woman sprang from a parapet upon the bridge-head and darted in front of the oncoming horses. White Syrie snorted and shied, almost catching Richard unawares, for Syrie was a well-trained beast, and not liable to sudden restiveness or fear; Richard's favourite steed, chosen for his trustworthy nature. As the King struggled to bring the horse under control, the stallion backed up almost to the retaining wall, and Richard's spur struck the age-pocked stone, causing sparks to fly into the air.

The crone who had caused the commotion began to laugh, her voice thin and harsh, the cawing of a crow. Around her, the excited buzz of the throng died away, replaced by a strange hush, then a flurry of anxious whispers.

Richard stared down from Syrie at the woman. She was mad…she had to be mad. It must be her age, or perhaps drink or the hot sun had addled her mind. She appeared to be a washer-woman or a dyer, for she was wet and slimy from the river and held a man's shirt in the crook of her bony arm. The linen shirt dripped, dyed scarlet, and in its sopping state appeared to be leaking blood. The crone's visage was horrible, a jaundiced skull void of teeth, and she had but one eye, partly covered by a blue caul. Raising her free arm, she pointing at Richard with a gnarled finger caked with grime and cackled, "As your spur smote the stones of Bow Bridge so shall your head when you return, King Richard, third of that unlucky name!"

A gasp came from the crowd—harsh, audible. It was treasonous to ill-wish the King or to predict his demise. Immediately soldiers lunged forward and grasped the crazed old woman by the shoulders, hauling her roughly away from Richard. She continued to cackle, the blood-hued shirt slapping against her thin, wretched frame.

Some of the onlookers began to wail and howl, pushing forward toward the soldiers and waving their fists at the old crone. "Stone her, duck her... that's old Agnes Black, they say she has the gift of foresight, they say she's a witch!"

"Your Grace, what do you wish us to do with her?" asked the soldier who held the aged woman, sword held to her skinny throat.

"Nothing..." Richard was pale and stern-faced but seemingly unmoved by Agnes Black's wild prophecy. "I do not kill women. Especially old mad women, afflicted in the sight of God. Release her."

Reluctantly the guards let go of Agnes Black's bony arms. She turned to Richard, head twisting to one side, looking like some bird of prey gazing at a tender morsel.

"Men will say you are a tyrant," she cackled, "but perhaps you were too lenient, and that will be your undoing! Watch for he who consorts with one who has already betrayed you once, the spawner of dragons!"

"Old woman...Agnes Black, if that is indeed your name..." Richard leaned over the mane of White Syrie and stared solemnly into that livid face. "I do not know of what you speak. Nor do I wish to. Leave my presence before I change my mind about your fate."

Agnes Black slung her gory-hued rags over her shoulder in a welter of red droplets and hopped over the end of the bridge, surprisingly spry for one of such age. She landed in a crouch in the trampled mud below and began to stomp down the riverbank, cackling and gibbering to herself, while the throngs of watching townsfolk parted in disgust around her.

Richard turned White Syrie's head and looked away from the hag. He would be glad to leave Leicester. Glad to go into the countryside and meet his enemy, the self-proclaimed Lancastrian heir, Henry Tydder. The bastard who would style himself king.

Chapter Four—THE LAST BATTLE

Richard's great army headed out across the bridge in a stream of vibrant banners—the flags of England and St George, the Lions and Lilies, the White Boar—and marched briskly towards Redemore accompanied by the blare of trumpets and the beating of drums. This was to be the place of reckoning, where the King would stop Tudor from marching on towards London. Stop him forever.

Along the way the army passed myriad hamlets and villages where peasants worked the fields, stopping their toil to stare with the same expressions of mixed excitement and fear that Richard had seen in Leicester and Nottingham. Once again, he warned his men that there was to be no destruction of the crops these simple folk cultivated; the soldiers and the baggage trains would skirt the edges of the fields, even if it meant the journey was delayed. Any reports of damage or looting that reached the King's ears would be dealt with severely.

Riding close to Richard's side, Francis Lovell sighed. "It would be swifter, your Grace, if we did just ride through the crops and make restitution to the farmers after this matter is done."

"No," Richard said firmly, glancing at Francis out the corner of his eye. "Have you not heard? Tydder's foreign rabble have already been trampling the fields, uncaring that it might mean starvation for those who depend on them. I would not be seen to be like him…I am *not* like him."

"I know," said Francis, with a weary smile. This was the man, after all, who had once told a town 'I would rather have your love than your money' when they offered him the accustomed monetary gift. Of course, Richard would not ruin the fruits of his people's labour just to throw them a few coins in compensation when the strife was over.

As the army of the King continued on its journey, Richard passed close to one village with a mill and a green. The crops grew near to the edge of the old rutted road—sweet corn, ripened, ready for the harvest. The lines of corn tossed in the warm breeze, shining like a maiden's golden hair. The villagers were out amongst the fields with honed sickles, and as they worked, bending and swaying, arms rising and falling in rhythm, they sang an old song of the harvest,

'There were three kings from the west,
Three kings both great and high,
And they have sworn a solemn oath
John Barleycorn should die.

They took a plough and ploughed him down,
Laid clods upon his head,
For they have sworn a solemn oath
John Barleycorn was dead.

They've taken a weapon, long and sharp,
And cut him by the knee;
Then tied him fast upon a horse,
Like a rogue for sorcery.

They laid him down upon his back,
And cudgelled him full sore;
They hung him up before the storm,
And turned him o'er and o'er.

And they have wrest his heart's blood,
And drank it round and round;
And still the more and more they drank,
Their joy did more abound.

John Barleycorn was a hero bold,
Of noble enterprise;
For if you do but taste his blood,
'Twill make your courage rise....

It will make your courage rise!'

A scrap of cumulus scudded over the sun's burning disc and the landscape turned dim, dappled with cloud-shadows. Other clouds swept in from the west, anvil-shaped domes that dominated the horizons like siege-towers. Thunder rumbled in the distance and an unnatural yellowish light spread across the fields.

A summer storm was coming, fierce and terrible. The smell of warm rain flooded down the rising breeze. Horses skittered and hair stood on end, sharp with static. The east was a bruise, turning purple, then black.

Richard glanced at the sky, worried, and then turned in his saddle to face Francis Lovell. "I do not wish to ride through a storm. Is there any place nearby where we might find shelter?"

"I will find out, sire." Lovell beckoned a scout to his side and spoke earnestly to the man before sending him out on horseback across the dimming rises and hollows of the land.

The scout returned before long, riding hard on his fleet mare. The first raindrops were dappling his harness, damping down the dust of the road. "Over yonder, my Lords, is the village of Elmesthorpe. There is an old church, St Mary's, that lies partly in ruin, your Grace—its nave is sound and could provide some shelter from the storm."

Richard nodded; the yellow light was becoming thick, sickly, a jaundiced cap of unbridled power, falling to darkness where the clouds were thickest, swirling and rising like living beings. In the distance lightning crackled, sizzling over the trees in snarled masses. "Ride on for this Elmesthorpe," he commanded. "The storm is coming fast."

The King's army reached the village of Elmesthorpe just as the rain started to lash. The entire sky was now a roiling mass of black and yellow, shot through with spears of lightning. The village itself was partly deserted, humps and bumps in the ground showing that it must have once been much larger; like many English villages, the Black Death had ravaged its population in the last century. A few cottages clustered around a small manor house where, Richard's runners had told him, the sympathies of the tenants lay with Lancaster. The manor doors would be opened only unwillingly, if not barred altogether, and it was not worth starting a skirmish to take the house when good men and even more precious time might be lost. The church, St Mary's, stood at the end of the village's main street; it lay in partial ruin, a ragged line of skeletal arches gleaming against the threat of the thunder-laden sky.

Richard rode up to the gaunt and broken archways, twined with ivy fronds that blew straight out from the masonry in the howling gale. "*St Mary's*," he murmured.

Slight unease gripped him in this desolate place, but even this meager shelter was preferable to battling the thunder and lightning. Dismounting Syrie, he handed his reins over to his attendants and walked towards the undamaged part of the church, with its crenellated tower and great rusty bells swinging in the storm-wind. Warm raindrops lashed his face, stinging, slicking his hair to his cheeks.

Casting open the iron-bound door, he entered the musty darkness of the truncated nave, which smelled faintly of dampness, rotten wood, stale incense. His boots made loud clicking noises as he crossed the dank flagstones. He knelt before the altar, the strange storm-light pouring through the fragments of ancient glass in the windows, surrounding him in a surreal nimbus as he asked blessing on his men and forgiveness for using this hallowed soil for reasons of war.

As he knelt, head bowed, outside he could hear his men gathering in the lee of the walls. Their voices, muffled, slid like daggers through the cracked stonework; they spoke of the strangeness suddenness of the storm, the ominous hue of the sky. He heard talk of evil omens. Of doubt. He could sense their fear, a wavering in their resolve...

He closed his eyes, screwing them tightly shut. This church's dedication was to Mary, the Blessed Virgin, to whom he had particular devotion. He tried to pray to her for mercy and guidance but there seemed emptiness, a strange hollowness, in this half-destroyed building that made any prayer null and void, a whisper that reached no one.

The walls suddenly twisted away around him, bending like wheat before the wind, engulfed in the sick jaundiced light. They seemed to shimmer and he felt he was elsewhere...not in a church, but in a fallow field, with a starless sky above, a hard dome that stretched into infinity. It was not dark, yet not light either, and there was no moon and no sun, although no clouds drifted across the heavens to conceal them. A wind blew, rushing through dry grasses with an eerie rustling sound. Beneath that unfriendly sky, a woman was standing beside a rough-hewn stone, her back towards him, singing softly the well-known words of the Corpus Christi carol:

"Lulley, lully, lulley, lully,
The falcon has born my mate away.
He bore him up, he bore him down,
He bore him into an orchard brown.
In that orchard there was an hall,
That was hanged with purple and pall.
And in that hall there was a bed,
It was hanged with gold so red.
And in that bed their lieth a knight,
His wounds bleeding day and night.
By that bedside kneeleth a maid,
And she weepeth both night and day.
And by that bedside there standeth a stone,
"Corpus Christi" was written thereon."

From the back, Richard could see that the woman was slim, with fairish, loose hair unconcealed by any headdress. Her tresses hung to her hips, shining faintly in the strange half-light of that twilit land, while an immodest transparent shift fluttered round bare ankles. For a second, she seemed somehow familiar. Maybe it was the hair, or the slenderness, the familiar grace…. "Anne?" he said querulously, his voice catching in his throat.

The woman turned toward him, resting her slender hand upon the standing stone. He could see now that she was most definitely not Anne; indeed, he had never seen her before, despite that instant of familiarity.

It was perplexing and frightening, gazing into that still, pale face; one moment she reminded him of Jane Shore, his brother's harlot, who he had punished by making her walk the streets of London wearing just a shift, a taper gripped in her hand; the next the hated Woodville woman with her silver-gold hair and calculating dragon's eyes. The woman he was sure was a witch, who had ensorcelled Edward into wedding her and who had cast a web over Richard himself in June of

1483, making his sword arm feel weak, his breathing tight and his heart a thundering drum. He had accused Elizabeth Woodville of sorcery on that horrible day when Hastings had drawn weapons in the council chamber...but no formal charge had ever been made against her.

The fair-haired female took a step in his direction and he now noticed that she wore a crown, its tines tipped by what seemed to be stars, shimmering and glittering like no earthly stones. Her face looked different again; serene and still as marble, having neither Jane's over-ripe wantonness, nor Elizabeth Woodville's arrogance. It was the face of a Queen, but scarcely a human face, changing, as it did, like the phases of the moon.

Dropping to one knee in the grass, he bowed his head. "Lady, surely you must be the very Queen of Heaven, though I did not recognize you at first with my sinner's eyes."

"The Queen of Heaven?" Her voice emerged from her pale, pale lips, echoing and strange. "Some have called me such. Others the Queen of Hell. But I am not the Queen you think me, not the blue-robed Mother. My robes are more often green...green, the colour of life but also the grass that grows on men's graves..."

"Who are you then, if not the Blessed Virgin? Are you some sorceress, sent to beguile me? What is your name?" He rose and approached her slowly, fingers curling round the hilt of his dagger. "Give me your name. I demand it. I am the King."

She smiled, and it seemed all darkness stretched within the caverns of her eyes. He could not tell what colour they were; they looked black, pupiless, unnatural eyes. "One day you will know it, Richard Plantagenet. But if you know it not now, I may not tell you."

A hissing sound filled the surrounding landscape like the sound of escaping marsh gasses. In an eye's blink, the fey woman was gone, and the heavy, still sky over them both was crumbling inwards, piece by piece, like soil falling into a grave...

Richard jolted upright, tense, alert as if he expected an enemy to attack. It was as if he had woken from a nightmare but it was a waking dream, if that were so; he still knelt before the altar of St Mary's. The rood screen glistened dully in front of him, green gold in the storm-light. Carved roof bosses grinned down at him, as if enjoying his discomfiture.

After a few minutes of disorientation, he came fully to himself, his breathing growing less ragged, the gallop of his heartbeat slowing. He glanced around. The vision, if that is what it was, had dissipated utterly; everything in the ruined church was as it should be. He crossed himself, ashamed to have had thoughts of that sinister, immodestly clad female while seeking the blessings of God. Maybe he should have asked one of his men to head out and find some camp-follower for him; many men sought out the pleasures of a leman in the last hours before a battle. It would shock many members of his retinue; he had been known for the goodness of his private life with Anne and had openly condemned the lax morality of Edward's court.

But Anne was dead these past five months...and no, he had not been bedding his niece, as the gossips whispered. Elizabeth may have been infatuated with him; he did not know or care. Certainly she wept loudly enough when, burning with shame, he publicly declared that he had no designs on her, and her tears fell even harder when he sent her from London to the children's nursery hundreds of miles away at Sheriff Hutton.

He smiled grimly. No, he would not compound his sins by seeking out the coarse and venal. Unlike Edward, he could master his own flesh. He would go to this battle for his crown as close to a pure knight as one such as he could ever be. When the struggle was over, he would marry the Princess Joanna and unite the House of York and Lancaster in honour and dignity.

*Soon...*Once this matter with Henry Tydder was over, and he had killed the swivel-eyed pretender who made the outrageous claims, *"I am of King Arthur's line!"* or *"I am in truth the son of Henry VI!"* Richard would have the matter of the Portuguese marriage attended to immediately. If God willed it, soon after there might be another prince of the

House of York in the cradle, filling that awful void left by the death of young Ned.

May God will my victory and be with me on the morrow, he thought, and he walked out of that desolate church and into the crash of the storm.

The inclement weather lasted several more hours, a cataclysm in the sky that vanished almost as quickly as it came, one final display of dazzling lightning, then the thunderheads retreating over a low line of distant hills. Red and ragged, the sun emerged again and the heat of summer returned. Steam rose in clouds from the drenched land.

Richard and his army moved on from Elmesthorpe church, the King glad to leave its gaunt arches and their unsettling memories behind him. After a few miles had passed, in the distance he spied a hill rising out of the flat vista. A single tree crowned its summit, high above the others that grew in snarled clumps on its flanks, a dark silhouette against the dusky blue of the summer sky. The tree had strangeness about it, and against his will, he remembered the oak tree in Bestwood decked with its gory fruit, the Hanged Man that yet spoke. But that was surely just an evil dream, a fancy born of a strange summer's afternoon of fog and shade and too-bright sun...

"Where is that place?" Richard asked his secretary John Kendall, who rode on his left amongst others of his household. He shaded his eyes with a hand against the brightness, scanning the wooded hill. "Do you have any idea, John?"

"It should be Ambien Hill according to the maps, Your Grace," came the reply. The older man's eyes teared as he strained into the bright distance. "The enemy is not far from us now."

"Near that hill and its single tree is where we will make our camp for the night," said Richard quietly, determinedly, "before facing Henry Tydder at the dawn."

The King's army camped all across the high hill and across the rolling land around it; tents billowed in the wind, banners flew, snapping on the breeze; the sounds of vast moving hordes of men and beasts filled the summer air—horses neighing, men singing , drums beating. Richard had his tent set up not far from the small hamlet of Sutton Cheney, with its squat, ancient church of St James tucked away in a low, grassy churchyard. His informants came with the news that Tydder's forces had taken over Atherstone after causing further damage in the fields of Fenny Drayton, the uncaring mercenaries laughing as they crushed the corn into the dust and molested the local women.

As the sun slipped westwards, the sky melted to blood and small campfires began to glow across the gently undulating landscape—the very heart of England, the centre of the realm, where the slow heart of ancient Albion beat slowly in time with the change of seasons, the passage of untold years. In the distance, the campfires of Henry Tudor's men flickered like corpse-candles, dancing in the growing twilight. Strands of smoke rose from them like spectral hands snatching at a prize...at Richard's crown, at the life's blood of England itself. The heavy, languorous air reeked with the scent of burning wood.

Inside Richard's fine pavilion, painted with his colours and mottoes, with great bristling boars guarding the tent-flaps and the White Rose of York flowering above the door, the King gathered for a council of war with the most important men of his realm—Francis Lovell, Dick Ratcliffe and William Catesby, Brackenbury, John Howard Duke of Norfolk, a sullen and uneasy Henry Percy, and many other notables. Between discussions of weaponry, artillery and stratagems of war, they dined richly on goose, swan, and boar, and fine wine was passed around, and occasionally, between the solemnities, there was even some laughter amidst the lords, though Richard seemed quieter than usual, listening to the speeches of others more than joining in. Many words of bravado were spoken, especially as the wine flowed, but on this occasion, the King did not speak these words himself.

He would win on the morrow; he had to believe in that. God would finally smile on him and give him the right. He had the greater forces, the better artillery. The Stanleys were a problem—Sir William had gone over to Tudor but the equally fickle Thomas was lurking on the edges of the field, undeclared…but Richard had something that he hoped might stay his hand should Tydder's step-father start to waver. He held Thomas's son, Lord Strange, as a prisoner, and he hoped the threat of execution hovering above Strange's head would be enough to deter Thomas Stanley from treasonous actions.

Shortly before midnight, he bade farewell to his friends and captains and bid them rest before the hard day that followed. John Howard and Francis Lovell were the last of that great company to leave the royal tent; John, a grey-haired and moustached man of about sixty, clasped his kinsman's hand and squeezed it firmly. Although considerably older than Richard, they had always held great affection for each other. The choice of name for Richard's illegitimate son John had come through his friendship with the man his called 'beloved cousin.'

"We will see this through, Dickon," John Howard said, but a look of worry darkened his eyes.

Richard chewed on his lip, as he often did when he was uneasy. He could read the apprehension in John's face and it disturbed him. "What is wrong, my kinsman?" he asked quietly. "Hold nothing from me, this night of all nights."

John Howard took a deep breath. "I found a note…pinned to my tent. Who put it there, I cannot say, but its very appearance tells me that there are traitors and troublemakers in our midst!"

"What did this note say?" Richard's voice was flat, cold.

John Howard pulled out a crumpled shred of parchment and read off it in a low voice: '*Jockey of Norfolk, be not so bold, for Dickon thy master is bought and sold.*"

An uncomfortable silence descended over the tent. Lovell looked shocked. Richard's visage was unreadable, his face like carven granite, white between the dark wings of his hair.

Then, suddenly, he threw back his head and laughed. "Doggerel. And this is the worst they can throw at us?" Despite his seeming mirth, he toyed with the dagger at his side, a nervous gesture that he often did without thinking. "Well, whoever wrote this would do well to remember Colyngbourne and the consequences of his treasonous little poem…and his spying for Henry Tydder."

"I will see to it that there are added men on watch, in case our 'poet' returns and tries to add another verse," said Howard, with a grim smirk, ripping up the note and flinging the scraps onto the brazier.

"On the morrow then," said Richard. "We will have proper ballads written about us when it is all over. And good Master Caxton shall print them. That's if he ever gets over me parting his patron Anthony Woodville from his head."

John Howard hurried off into the darkness and the smoke of the fires, leaving Richard alone with Francis Lovell. Here, out of sight of the others they were as two old friends, not so much king and subject…just friends who had known each other since boyhood, who knew each other's deepest fears and secrets.

"Well, by tomorrow night, God willing, we will not have Henry Tudor to worry about any longer," said Francis. "We should prevail, even though the Stanleys bring me discomfort. There are a lot of men with them, and with Thomas undeclared…"

"They bring me discomfort too," said Richard, crossing his arms across his chest and staring into the darkness gathering beyond the entrance of the tent. "When I took Lord Strange as hostage and told his father of his fate if he betrayed me, do you know what Thomas said? 'I have other sons.' They do as they wish, the Stanleys, always swinging in the wind like corpses upon a gallows."

"Which is where I'd like to see them," said Francis. with a snort of mirth. "On a gallows."

"So would I!" Richard grinned, letting his arms drop back to his side. "Some men say I am hard. But perhaps with that family I have not been hard enough!"

The two men both laughed, though their laughter held a touch of false bravado, the faintest undertone of a dawning doubt too awful to dwell upon. The two Stanley brothers had huge personal armies between them, enough that they could potentially swing the outcome of the battle. One had already shown his true colours, though none knew what action he might take on the morrow. And the other…unknown….

Richard's face suddenly grew somber, serious. "Frank…" he used Lovell's childhood name, "I…I thank you for remaining loyal to me. Even when I was a fool and was gulled by the snake's tongue of Buckingham, you did not waver, did not turn from me. No matter what happens tomorrow, know you that my gratitude will always be there, in this life and beyond it."

"You are my friend as well as my King…How could I not stand by you?" Francis sank to one knee, overcome by a sudden swell of emotion—and a sudden awful prescience of what might come with the dawn. Clumsily he grasped Richard's hand and kissed it.

"Get up, Francis." Richard said hoarsely; he gestured his friend to his feet. "No need…"

Francis's voice broke. "To my ears it sounded as if you were saying… farewell. As if you thought you might…" He could not finish, his words strangling in his throat.

Richard glanced at him, wondering to see his friend so overcome. "Don't be ridiculous, Frank. Where did you get such an idea? Now, come, wish me a good night and let me go to my couch, you know I do not sleep well."

Francis rose and he and Richard hugged awkwardly and stood there, almost as if unwilling to let each other go; and for a moment Richard laid his head against his friend's shoulder as if willing him to give him strength and support.

The King's face was pale, clear, in the flickering candle light, almost as if lit from within; but Francis noted it was also translucent-pale, like Anne's had been before she died; tired and worn but strangely arresting, almost the face of a war-like angel, a St Michael who was facing the dragon in a fight to the death. It was a fey look that clung to Richard Plantagenet, as if he were no longer of mortal earth, and again

Lovell had the dreadful sensation that together they teetered on the edge of something great and terrible that would draw them both in, a fate from which neither could escape.

Richard drew away first, moving towards his couch, his face averted from his friend. "Before dawn then, Frank," he said softly.

"Aye, I will be with you, Lord." Lovell fled the King's tent.

Richard roused himself before the dawn. Lying still for a moment beneath the covers on his couch, he listened to the sounds of his great army stirring all around him, just waking. The world seemed almost anew in the encroaching dawn, a time of reflective innocence before the rigors of the day were to begin. Sitting up, he called for his squires to bring him a robe. Holding it tightly round his shoulders, he walked to the entrance of his tent and gazed into the sky, just starting to lighten in the East. The Morning Star blazed on the horizon, white fire, like one of the jewels in his crown—a jewel in the crown of heaven.

He thought suddenly how some called this star the sigil of Lucifer and he shivered and turned back into the safe darkness of his tent. He could not dwell on any darkness, not on this day of reckoning.

Opening his Book of Hours, which accompanied him on all his campaigns, he mouthed the words of his personal prayer, his breath a soft rush, "Most Merciful Lord Jesus Christ as Thou didst wish to relieve those burdened with sore afflictions, to redeem the captives, to free the imprisoned, to bring together those who are scattered, to restore the contrite in heart, to comfort the wretched, and to console those who grieve and mourn, deign to release me from the affliction, temptation, grief, infirmity, poverty and peril in which I am held, and give me aid. Extend Thine arm to me; pour Thy grace over me, and free me from all the distresses and griefs by which I find myself troubled.

"Thou saidst "Oh Lord, it is finished...." Richard halted abruptly at this line, his eyes growing damp with unforeseen emotion; he could see his squires staring through the gloom, alarmed. It was as if something held him back from completing the prayer, something deep inside his mind that told him beyond any doubt...

It is finished.

After he had been dressed and made ready, the King went to mass with his captains at St James' church. Dewdrops on the grass sparkled like tears and the glass in the arched windows shone with almost preternatural brightness as the rim of the sun lifted above the mist-capped trees and filled the world with rose-gold light. To Richard, everything seemed sharp and bright, strangely focused and clear—the colours streaking the sky, the grey church walls patched with lichen, the rich green grass in the churchyard dappled with wild flowers. Fragrances too, overwhelming—the rich aroma of damp earth, the green smell of the grasses, the scent of incense drifting from within the church nave. He had never noticed this 'aliveness,' this awareness, so strongly before a battle before, not at Barnet, nor Tewkesbury, nor at Berwick where he fought the Scots. He wondered what it could betoken. Everything suddenly seemed both beautiful and terrifying; this was his kingdom, and worth fighting for, and so easily it could slip away from him. But by God, it was his right to rule, and he would die before he let that Pretender claim his throne.

Once Mass had been said, the King's army began its march to the chosen site for the battle with the upstart Welshman Tudor. Banners unfolded, catching the light; early brightness glinted on armour, turning it to flame. Drums beat and in the distance, Tudor's men matched the sounds with a steady drumbeat of their own. The priests walked alongside the soldiers, holding up a great processional cross, finely wrought and decorated with gems—a symbol of hope to the King and his men.

Fenn Lane, the old Roman road, stretched out before the army, a straight white ribbon that vanished into the early morning haze. Riding on White Syrie, Richard led his men, while the ever-loyal Brackenbury took charge of the household troops, filled by stalwart men such as Ratcliff, Lovell and Catesby, John Kendal, Marmaduke Constable, Edward Redeman and others. Sir Percival Thirlwall bore aloft the Royal standard, uncurling and fluttering in the warm breeze that already promised a day of unbridled summer heat. The Duke of Norfolk led the archers, good stout men bearing longbows as tall as or taller than they were.

Richard had earlier donned his expensive armour, crafted to his specifications to support the curve of his spine. Upon his helmet, he wore a ceremonial crown, its golden tines burning like flames in the burgeoning sunlight, marking out his presence to friend and foe alike, a statement of his right and his royalty…but also making him an obvious target to his enemies.

Raising his visor, he surveyed the landscape, the glowing green of the fertile fields and the swampy marshlands around Redemore Dyke, heavy with the reek of stagnant water. A nearby low-slung hill seemed to bleed red—its flank heaved with Stanley's crimson-clad men, like a mass of crawling ants.

At the sight of the traitor's forces, a flame of anger kindled inside him, twisting at his innards. He knew William Stanley's position and, by God, he was growing increasingly sure of Thomas's too. Turning sharply in the saddle, he beckoned Catesby over to him and said roughly, "Lord Strange…his father will betray us, I am certain of it. Have him executed."

"My lord?" Catesby looked alarmed by this sudden brutal command.

Richard's lips tightened and fire flashed in his eyes at Catesby's momentary hesitation, then, suddenly, he sighed, shook his head and raised a dismissive hand. "No, forget my words, I spoke in haste. There is no time for such business. Later, I will deal with the traitor's son, and hopefully Thomas Stanley too."

A sudden fluttering noise sounded in the sky above and a hush fell over the assembled soldiers. The first arrows.

Norfolk's men had released them towards the opposing forces of the experienced Oxford. The sound of the artillery fire began, blasting into the morning. Foul-smelling smoke belched from the cannon and birds rose shrieking in terror from the trees. Oxford's men began to change their formation, to one surrounded by a wall of deadly pikemen, while Norfolk's archers returned a volley of arrows that darkened the morning sky.

So it had begun.

Suddenly there was a flurry of commotion in Norfolk's ranks, and signs of the front lines wavering and breaking in some kind of alarm. More arrows flew from both sides, but most of the shafts went wide, skittering harmlessly along the ground.

"What is happening?" Richard's attention focused on the shift in the position of the men; a feeling of ominous dread clutched at his innards. Where was the loyal Duke of Norfolk? Why were the men breaking ranks and milling about aimlessly like cattle?

Moments later a shout came from behind; a messenger on horseback in Norfolk's colours, bringing news. "Your Grace…your Grace…Norfolk is down!"

"Down!" Richard's voice was harsh, strangling in his throat. "What do you mean? Speak clearer, man!"

"My Lord of Norfolk is dead, your Grace; struck in the eye by an arrow while in battle with De Vere. He raised his visor for one moment to survey the scene and a stray shaft smote him."

Richard fell silent, staring into the distance, his eyes growing ice-cold even as his face grew pale, colourless. Evil news, but he must hold firm; Norfolk's son Surrey would take over his slain father's position. "There will be retribution for this deed," he murmured.

It was important now to engage; the King knew he could not let his men think too much on this early loss of one of his staunchest supporters. Without preamble, he ordered his men to march forward with speed and take on the enemy. The marsh loomed up, rushes waving on the ragged edges, its tepid water glinting under the strengthening sun. Henry

Percy's men clustered nigh to its edge, having marched almost into its rancid borders, but now they stood motionless, like chess pieces upon a board waiting for some hand to guide them.

"What are those bastards doing?" Lovell hissed between gritted teeth, nodding in the direction of Percy's soldiers. "Dickon, I do not like the smell of this…"

"No time to worry about Northumberland, it is the time to act and finish this day!" Richard nodded toward the thinly-wooded hill where the Stanley brothers lurked with their troops; he could see their banners, one bearing the heads of harts, reminding him of the antlered man who had appeared to him in Bestwood, and the other broidered with cruel clawed eagles—those over-proud birds of prey that tore flesh with beak and claw.

For the moment, the turncoat brothers were safely on the far side of the marsh, but Richard was under no illusion they would remain so for long. "Linger too long and Thomas Stanley might definitely throw in his lot with his brother, as we have all feared he might. But…if I can bring down Tydder, or put him to flight, then Thomas Stanley might stay his hand, even though the Welsh bastard is his step-son…you know how the Stanleys always like to have one brother on each side of a battle, to plead the case for the other one in the aftermath."

Francis shifted uneasily in the saddle. "What are you proposing, Richard?"

"I am going to hunt down Henry Tydder" Richard's eyes glittered through the thin slit of his visor, hard blue-grey diamonds. "See him over there, around the side of the marsh, with his guards circling him, the coward! I am going to finish the day with no more delay. We ride to take down this fraud, this impostor who brings his foul foreign mercenaries to rend the soil of England!" His voice was rising, full of anger, full of determination. He pulled White Syrie's head round; the great war-horse danced and trembled, feeling its master's impatience, his fury and power. *"Are you with me?"*

"I am always with you!" shouted Francis, though his heart was lurching, and a sick fear he had never felt before brought the taste of bile to his lips.

"Charge! *On On!*" Richard slammed his heels into Syrie's flanks and the horse sprang forward, white and gleaming like some mythical beast from legend. The household knights raced after the King, a stream of about a thousand men, thundering round the sodden edge of the marshland toward the spot where Henry Tudor hid amongst his knights and the clustered French and Swiss mercenaries he had brought with him.

Richard was riding too fast; he vaguely knew it but adrenaline shot through him, driving him on, erasing any fear. He was outstripping his household knights, riding Syrie like the wind. Ahead, he could see Tudor's bodyguard clearly; amidst their clustered ranks, he spied a lanky figure wearing the undifferenced Arms of England, which heightened Richard's righteous fury—the Welsh bastard had no right to such a device. As if sensing the proximity of his would-be slayer, Tudor's helmeted head turned in his direction, bobbed nervously, and then ducked down behind a sea of pikes.

The coward!

Richard galloped straight towards the spot where the gangling figure had vanished. A huge mounted knight, massive as a mountain, appeared from nowhere to block him; he recognized the colours as belonging to the veritable giant, Sir John Cheyney. With an oath, he drove at the giant with his lance; the impact against Cheyney's armour broke the tip asunder and the huge man cartwheeled through the air before crashing to the ground, semi-conscious, as blood oozed through gaps in his helmet.

Richard cast the broken lance aside and freed his battle-axe, striking around him with all the force of his rage. The flashing blade clove heads, arms, torsos, shearing through even the best armour with the fury of his assault; screams rang out, inhuman in their intensity, while blood fountained through the air, turning the scent of the morning from grass and growing things to cold iron and death.

Directly in front of Richard was Tudor's banner bearer, William Brandon, made a knight by his master that very day...a man of ill repute who had spent time in prison for raping a gentlewoman and her eldest daughter, and attempting to defile the younger. Brandon tried vainly to defend Tudor's banner but Richard was like an avenging fury bearing down upon him; his axe-blade smashed into the other man with the force of a thunderclap, cleaving his breast plate in twain and killing him instantly. Brandon fell, showering his life's blood, and the coils of Tudor's banner tumbled through the sky, the red dragon of Cadwallader crumpling to the ground, besmirched with the blood of the slain standard-bearer.

By now, Richard's household knights were gaining on their King, hurling themselves against the lines of the enemy force protecting Henry Tudor. If Tudor could be killed, it would be all over; the battle over with its figurehead gone. Suddenly a cry went up: "Stanley! Look to Stanley!"

Richard glanced quickly to one side. Sir William Stanley had moved; his forces were plunging into the fray, eager to protect Tudor. Although Thomas Stanley remained motionless on his horse, some of his men were joining in with William's, swelling their numbers. Like a surging tidal wave, the traitors' forces slammed into Richard's band of knights, throwing them into disarray and driving them back toward the edge of the foetid marsh.

Everything was changing.

Sir Percival Thirlwall, Richard's standard-bearer, went down first. An axe-blow took him at the knees, severing both legs. He did not scream, even as his life left him; his body still lurched forward on bloodied stumps, trying to hold his lord's precious standard aloft. But then he pitched forward into the trampled mud, and Richard's banner sank down over his corpse, the proud Boar snarling impotently as it fell to earth.

A mercenary charged out of the ranks of Tudor's guard and thrust a long pike at Richard's mid-section, attempting to unseat him or find a chink in his armour. The man's movements were slow, the sticky ground impeding his rush, and the King struck him with his battle-axe, cleaving his skull in twain with one lethal blow. The mercenary fell, and was replaced by a dozen other enemy soldiers who thrust their spears and pikes at Richard's horse, seeking to bring the beast to his knees and get to his rider. Syrie was as well armoured as his master, but Richard took no chances of the attackers finding an unprotected area of the beast's body and skillfully wheeled the stallion out of the way with his free hand tightly gripped upon the reins.

Suddenly Syrie, usually so sure-footed and reliable, stumbled and his hind quarters buckled under, causing Richard to jolt forward in the saddle and almost lose grip on his weapon. The horse's eyes began to roll in fear and he tossed his great head and fought the bit. Richard stared down at the ground in dismay...he had unwittingly backed his steed into the cloying red soil on the periphery of the marsh, and it was sucking at Syrie's hooves and fetlocks, drawing the animal down, dragging him into the black heart of the marshes on Redemore Plain. He had to get him out, had to...*or*...*or*...

A shower of arrows darkened the morning sky and suddenly one bloomed in a small, unarmoured spot on Syrie's neck, its goose-feather fletchings quivering. The mighty war-horse fell like a stone, legs thrashing wildly. Richard managed to hurl himself away as the horse's body crashed into the mud, and using all the skills learned while under the tutelage of Warwick, managed with surprising agility to vault back up onto his feet before any foes had the chance to pin him down.

"*My God, I am unhorsed*!" he thought frantically, knowing what that could mean in a battle such as this one. It was common enough for nobles to fight each other on foot, but only if you were not isolated from your men. He stared around him, seeking for Francis, Ratcliffe...anyone. His rush had carried him far forward into the fray, leaving his followers behind; near him, he saw only the blood-hued Stanley colours and the hodge-podge of Tudor's ragged mercenaries, the rabble of France's gaols.

Suddenly through the heaving mass of men near Tudor's banner galloped Juan Salazar, a Spaniard sent by the King and Queen of Spain to assist the Yorkist side in the battle. He was dragging a horse by the bridle, as it fought against him, fearful of the blood-scent and the loud roars of the cannon, the hiss and shriek of arrows.

"Your Grace," he shouted, ploughing through the melee toward the horseless Richard. "We saw your mount go down! The battle goes against us! Here...I have brought another horse for you....take it and ride away to live and fight another day!"

"I will not!" Richard shouted back, appalled that any would expect he should flee the field. "God forbid I should yield a step. I will win or I shall die as King!"

The battle washed over them, and Salazar and his offer of a steed were swept away into the heart of the fighting, where William Stanley's men hacked and hewed with mad abandon, killing Ratcliffe and then Brackenbury, and sending others of Richard's men in a desperate rush for safety down Fenn Lane. John Kendall fell; his pen stilled by the mightier sword, while Francis Lovell disappeared in a crush of steeds, jostling men at arms and mounted knights. Foreign mercenaries were surrounding Richard now—pikemen and soldiers with bills and pollaxes, a few bearing swords and daggers. They formed a dark wall, closing in. "Treason!" he shouted, anger and despair rising up in him. "*Treason!*"

He suddenly knew then, in that moment. Knew the truth.

He was going to die.

It was a shock. Always there had been the chance of death, as with any battle, but his numbers surpassed Tydder's and his artillery more advanced. He had experience...his adversary had never fought a battle before. Deep inside, he had been convinced he would prevail, his right asserted, God granting him the opportunity to atone for sins of the past and be a good King to his people...

But it was not going to happen.

Around him, the battle surged, and he fought on instinctively, as his armour slowly began to fail, dented by many blows. Everything seemed to move in slow motion, seconds becoming as hours, with the sounds, the smells, the colours brighter, stronger, and clearer than before, even more radiant than earlier that morning. He thought of his family, of Anne and little Edward, both recently dead, so young, and of how he himself was not quite thirty-three years old... the same age Christ had been when he died upon the Cross. The comparison was sacrilegious but he knew, obliquely, that just as Christ made his sacrifice to save mankind, so he too would lay down his life for his people, a scapegoat taking away their sins with his death, ushering in a new golden age for England...an age that his killer and his successors would claim as their own. Caught in a cycle older than time, he was this day to make the Land, the beating red-stained heart of England, both Sacred and Profane.

Hands grappled with him, he felt himself driven to his knees. His weapons were torn from his hands. Someone cut the strap on his helmet and ripped it off, their knife nicking his cheek as they did so; he felt air caress his hot face and smelt the tang of his own blood. He heard a triumphant shout and saw the golden ceremonial crown he had worn on his helmet spin through the sky, a wheel of fire against the blue. And then there was a crack against the top of his head, hurling him face-down into the mud; not a fatal blow but enough to floor him; confused, he stared down, with double vision, at the blood-hued soil of Redemore welling between his fingers, mingling with the stream of scarlet from his cheek and from his scalp.

It would only be seconds now before the *coup de grace*—with inborn knowledge, he sensed the presence of the men milling behind him, readying themselves for the final rush, tense with blood-lust, eager to win fame for slaying a King. He almost laughed, but soil was in his mouth and blood where he had bitten his lip—even now that he was down and weaponless, the miscreants dared not face him head on, as though he, a small man with a body slight as a woman's and a back twisted by the curse of his youth, could take them all on and win if they dared to face him one on one.

He heard a rush of displaced air; his own breath rushed in his lungs, and almost simultaneously two weapons descended from above—a sword and a pollaxe, the first thrusting deep into his skull, the other shearing straight through the back of his head...

The light went out...

//He was alone, naked in the dark. There was a night sky with no moon, no stars above albeit there were no clouds. Fields surrounded him; he could hear wind but nothing else... Phosphorus streamed by him, green and eerie, rolling in great clouds...he had seem this place in a dream before, but this was no longer a dream...//

Before him, dancing before his petrified gaze, he could see a rotating tunnel lit by an inner light. Gazing down its length, he viewed Redemore Plain as if from a great height. His remaining men were fleeing towards Dadlington, pursued by Tudor's forces and being cut down without mercy as they struggled to get to safety.

He...his body lay on the grass, while laughing mercenaries stripped off his expensive armour and took bits as trophies. They were excited and raging with blood lust; they kicked their fallen foe, before heaving the naked corpse onto the back of a horse, with his head dangling down one side, and his legs the other. They continued to strike out at the body, even then, jeering at their slain enemy; one mercenary thrust his dagger into the dead man, cutting through the buttock to pelvis, as he slurred a lurid joke to his comrades. At this dishonourable action, even the man's companions seemed shocked and slunk away, scowling, sickened.

"Get away from there!" From where he watched at the end of the tunnel, Richard heard one of Tydder's captains roar at the out-of-control brigands. "Whatever you do, don't touch his fucking face! Don't touch it, you scum, or there will be hell to pay!"

The captain approached the dead king, tying a rope around the slain man's hands to bind him to the horse's saddle, then, smirking, knotted Richard's hair beneath his chin to help preserve the face that was so important for identification. This humiliation complete, he dragged forward Richard's herald, the young John Norrey, known as Blanc Sanglier, the White

Boar, and forced the boy up behind his dead master on the horse. Norrey stared down at the desecrated body of his King and burst into tears, sobs that shook his frame until he looked ready to collapse.

"You'll go to Leicester now, my boy!" the captain shouted at Blanc Sanglier." And you'll do your work as herald, proclaiming the death of this usurper, this crookback...' He glanced contemptuously at Richard's naked back, its right-sided curve made a hundred times more obvious by the bent position in which he lay. "And you'll tell them that King Henry, seventh of that name, heir to King Arthur himself and to the House of Lancaster, will soon be arriving in the town to greet his loyal subjects."

The tunnel Richard stared through to view these surreal and horrifying events was growing dim and receding even as he watched. The images of the battlefield began to waver and stream away, like ragged shreds of mist born on the wind. Richard, lost in this new dark land, stared, fixated, as Blanc Sanglier bore his body toward Leicester, surrounded by his adversary's crowing soldiers. Thomas Stanley, smug and flushed, was plucking Richard's crown from a thorn-bush that grew beside the marsh, and placing it reverently on the brow of the smirking, wispy-haired man that was Henry Tudor...

He wanted to scream but he could make no sound, seemed not to breathe. Aye, and so it was—how could he breathe, if he were dead?

He recoiled from the visions, staggering away into the darkness. He was dead, he knew it; he had seen sparks of light running down the honed edges of drawn blades, heard the whistle of cloven air as they slashed down...felt the hideous crunch of bone for one fleeting instant before blackness rushed in to claim him.

Yet how could he be dead and yet still have consciousness and an awareness of his fate? And if he *was* dead, he certainly had not ascended to Heaven... whatever the name of this strange, empty land, God was absent from it. Yet neither was he in Hell, the pit of torment he feared he might deserve—no flames spewed from gashes in the earth, and no demons capered screaming in delight as they thrust pitchforks into the flesh of sinners who burned for all eternity. No, there was just dimness and emptiness, the long field of blowing grass, the sunless and moonless sky, and a row of dark, featureless hills in the distance.

Suddenly he knew where his unearthly prison must be.

A place only slightly less fearsome than hell. A place where he might dwell for a thousand years yet never be deemed worthy enough to leave and enter God's kingdom…

Purgatory.

Chapter Five—THE MIDDLE KINGDOM

Richard wandered for a while, like a lost child. He would have wept but his eyes were dry…the dead cannot cry. Eventually he stumbled on a well; he remembered passing a similar one earlier in the day *'When I was alive!'* and tried to take a draught, but the water did not refresh, his throat remained tight and parched, wrenched with fear and grief.

Wandering even further afield, he found a stretch of water that glimmered low and dark in the perpetual twilight; a deep confluence of two rivers. He realized he was all covered with blood and mire, even as his body had been when it was flung across the horse with poor John Norrey up behind, and he leaped into the water to try and cleanse himself, to cleanse the awful memory of what had transpired that evil morning.

When he reached the other side of the tract of still, dark water, he was pleased to find his skin free of blood…and of wounds. He touched his face, his ribs, where he had taken knife cuts; there was nothing there now. Tentatively, fearfully, he stretched up to touch his head, which he knew had been shattered by sword and pollaxe.

Nothing.

No blood. No torn scalp. No matter from his brain running amidst the damp curling strands of his hair.

A sudden feeling of gratitude washed over him amidst his fear, and he sank into the long, growing grass, overcome. He knew he should not be happy, because this strangeness was not the reward a godly man should expect upon his death. But perhaps he had not been godly enough—despite recognizing his sins, despite repentance. But was he truly worse than all others, his sins at the utmost level? Was he to have allowed himself to be carried by the tides of war and smashed against the Woodvilles' shores without defending himself? Was he to have meekly offered up his own throat and that of Anne and Edward, like beasts to the slaughter, in order to see Edward's son crowned? He knew the lives of Lord Protectors were often brutally cut short as opposing factions warred over the control of a powerful minor…

He put his hands over his head. He must not think of his past any longer, it was all gone, all beyond him now. There was no heaven for him, no reunion with those he loved. Only this chilling world, caught 'tween dusk and dawn, where the wind always sighed and no stars shone.

He heard footsteps on the grass, above the soughing of the wind. Letting his hands drop he saw, standing by a single rowan tree, the woman who had appeared to him in the vision in Elmesthorpe church. Beautiful and yet sinister, she smiled at him and held out her pale thin hands—in each she held a sheaf of wheat. Her eyes were grave-dark, expressionless; her lips the blood upon the plain of Redemore. Her crown of stars now burned with candles, flicking and dancing like corpse-candles in a bog, the little lights that led unwary wanderers to their doom. She raised her left hand and let the wheat sheaf fall from it; it tumbled to the ground and was scattered to the blowing winds.

"So it is come to pass," she said. "Across the land in hamlet and hollow the villagers cut the last sheaves…one for Richard, one for Henry…one for Henry, one for Richard… And where the sickle cut closest, that one fell at the last, his body giving sustenance to the very heart of Albion. So is the ancient prophecy of Sandeford fulfilled, and the Red Dragon shall burn the land of England with his fiery breath."

"What prophecy is this?" Richard asked, frowning.

"One believed by your opponent, Henry of Richmond. One made long ago by Thomas of Ercildoune, known as true

Thomas, and then spoken again in these times by mad Robert Newton of Cheshire, who still lives, though he will meet his own doom in not so many years by hand of the Dragon's son..."

The Lady began to pace, and then to chant in a sing song voice:

"When a raven shall build in a stone lion's mouth
on a church top beside the grey forest
then shall a king of England be driven from his crown
and return no more
but he led in triumph by a Dragon
laid across a horse's back

A bitter Boar with main and might
shall bring a royal rout that day
there shall die many a noble knight
to be driven into fields green and grey-
they shall lose both field and fight

England shall be three times lost and won in one day
A crow shall sit atop the Headless Cross
by the marshes so grey
and drink of the noble's gentle blood so free

Many nobles shall fight
but a bastard Duke from the west shall win the day.
On the south side of Sandeford where lies a stone
where a crowned king will lose his head
and the Dragon gain renown

then the Eagle to an island shall retire
where leaves and herbs grow fresh and green
there he shall meet a lady fair
who counsels friends in battle slain

but after shall be better days
church and honest men onward living
and under the grey and fallen wall
shall be found the bones of a British king..."

"So you tell me all in England will go on as before, and there will be better days now that I am gone...and I...I am lost...lost forever, in this place, this purgatory! I almost wish there had been *nothing* after death!" Richard cried. "All is lost and it must ever be burned in my memory. And you...who are you to keep tormenting me? You witch, you heathen sorceress!"

"No witch am I." Her voice was stern, steel. "Neither of heaven nor of earth am I, or my People. We are of the Middle Kingdom, set between your Heaven and your Hell. I am she who spoke to True Thomas, Thomas the Rhymer, and put the Sacred Fire within his head and gave him the gift of prophecy. Mad Newton I also knew, taken with my nightly ride across the high cliffs at Alderley. Men who know me come away a poet or a madman, 'tis said—sometimes both." She laughed, her voice the tinkle of bells, of falling icicles, fair yet cold as winter. "I have many names and yet none. I am the Queen of fair Elfland, where this day you must go."

Richard stared at the woman, this self-styled Queen, in stricken silence. This was madness, and yet how could he, trapped in this unwholesome world, having experienced things he knew were impossible, condemn her words as a lie? Yes, the country folk still believed in elven folk, who lived in hollow hills where men's bones were found, but he was a modern man, an educated man, and had no belief in such creatures, not even when he had ridden late at night on the moors above Middleham and seen dancing lights and heard strange, drawn-out cries that came from no creature he could identify. If such creatures as elves walked earth, they were remnants from an old pagan time, fading from the world even in the age of Arthur, and as scripture made no mention of them, they were demons surely, sent by Satan to deceive...

The woman, the Elf-Queen, sighed languorously and gestured with impatience to Richard. "Shall you stand still as a stone pillar all night, pondering me and what I might betoken? All you have known is changed, changed utterly. A high destiny still lies before you, Richard Plantagenet, despite the earthly disaster that has befallen you this day. Come, you have bathed in the *halig-well*, the holy well that will bear your name forever more, and been cleansed and renewed in the waters of Scence the Shining One. Dress, my lord, and come hence with me without further delay..."

She held out a doublet of silver, spun of web-like cloth so fine it seemed as if a spider had woven it, and a cloak of leaf-green velvet, and green, pointed shoes too. Richard dressed swiftly, pleased at least by the sense of normality in the rich cloth touching his skin. For a brief moment, at least, he could forget the dreadful truth that threatened to overwhelm him, to make him mad...if insanity could overtake the restless dead.

The Lady took his hand, cold fingers twining with his as a vine twines about a stone, strangling it, swathing it. "You will, in this place, call me The Queen and nothing more, for of my many names I am all and none, as I am everything and nothing to all men."

They went through the twilight, the Lady, the Queen of Elfland, in the lead, moving like a fallen star across the glimmering plains. Eventually they reached a place where the path they traveled on diverged and branched out into three roads, one leading north, one east, and one west. The eastern road was tortuous and narrow, beset by briars and nigh impassable, while the one heading north was wide, plain and straight, gleaming welcomingly amidst a sea of white lily-flowers. The one to the west was twisted and winding, its edges brushed by ferns and blackthorn and whitethorn trees.

The Queen pointed to the three paths. "See you the road with its sharp thorns, leading through the mire? That is the Road to Righteousness; though after it but few inquire. And see you that broad white road, stretched out amid the lily-mead...Why, that is the road that leads to Hell, though some think of it as Heaven." She laughed, her voice rising like a clear bell above the constant soughing of the wind.

"And the third?" Richard asked. "What is the third? Where does it lead?"

"That fair and winding road that curves across the moor? That, my comely lord, is the road to bonny Elfland, where you and I this night shall go."

She guided him onwards, following the winding path beneath the canopy of faerie blackthorn and hawthorn, until they reached a hillock, a cairn of many stones, some cup-marked, others pecked out with zig-zags and spirals, which was surrounded by a low bank and ditch, an earth-ring of power, a circle that harnessed moon, and sun and earth. A crooked hawthorn crowned the faerie hill; this tall tree was full of unseasonable blossoms, their cloying scent permeating the air. Richard grimaced; he had always hated the perfume of the May Trees, sweet but deathly, like flesh in the first stages of decay. He could remember that sweet stench in his nostrils on the field at Tewkesbury on May 4, back in 1471, when York had won the day and the Lancastrian Prince of Wales, Anne's loathsome first husband, had died in the rout. Still so clear: the field men called Bloody Meadow, its grass awash with red life's blood and the May Trees overlooking all, the stench of their blossoms mingling with that of the gore and death rising around them…

The Queen of Elfland sat down daintily beneath the tree, circled by a ring of toadstools with spotted red caps; deadly poison, but strangely beautiful, compelling in the lavender light. Her skirts spread out around her, a glistening moon-circle under the moving sky, mirroring the circle bank around them. She beckoned Richard to sit at her side and he knelt upon those outspread skirts, awkwardly. The Queen touched the toadstools with her fingertips and suddenly in their place, Richard saw a loaf of bread and a flagon of claret resting upon a jewelled trencher.

"Eat and drink," ordered the Elf-Queen. "It is for you."

He was uncomfortable accepting sustenance from this strange being but felt compelled to do her bidding at the same time. Though the wine smelt fair and the bread was seemingly fresh, the liquid did not dampen his throat and the food tasted like ash, or like withered autumnal leaves, in his mouth.

It is not real food, he thought. *It is wrought by the glamour of faerie. And I…I am dead. Mortal pleasures are now beyond me for all that I can mimic them in this place of ungodliness. I know this…*

He wanted to weep then, but the dead cannot weep.

The Queen reached out and touched his face; her fingers were cool, strands of mist. "Do not sorrow. Join my band and you will dwell with me forever as a knight of Faerie. See what I can offer you?"

She raised an arm to the sky, and a yammering sound filled the heavens, the wild belling of hounds or migrating geese in winter—and Richard was reminded of childhood legends of the Wild Hunt, in which the devil himself, flaunting a pack of hell-hounds, chased souls of the wicked across the firmament before dragging them down into the fires.

Out of the west, pounding the clouds in their fury, rode a cavalcade of ghostly knights, fair and beautiful, on horses wrought of frothing cloud-stuff. Their hair flowed in the wind of their speed, dark as ebon, gold as sunbeams, and their armour was the hue of the vanquished moon that shone not in that desolate land of the Middle Kingdom. Green flames twined sword blades and lances, and coronets of stars shone on their brows. No blemish or imperfection stained them, in appearance, they were faultless as angels; Richard could see them in no other way, although he knew the bright troupe was of unholy origin not of God's making.

"Lady, you mock me." He tore his gaze from the vision in the sky. "I could not join such a company, even were it my choice to do so."

Her fair brows lifted. "And why is that? Why would you spurn my offer of eternity as one of the guardians of the unseen realm?"

"I have eyes that still can see...although I am dead," he spat with bitterness. "Whatever they may be in truth, the knights of your host are as fair as angels, and I....I...am..." He stared at the ground, hands clenched into fists.

"What are you, Richard Plantagenet?" asked the Queen of Faerie softly.

He reacted with wild fury. "Do not taunt me! You know! You have seen me unclothed. My shoulder, my back. Since I was a youth....Damn you, bitch, must you force me to say it? I am deformed!"

In answer to his impassioned outburst, the Elf-Queen laid her hands upon his shoulders and turned him so that he faced her straight on. She raised her mouth to his and her lips brushed against his, cold, faint, the kiss of mist. As with the faerie food, there was the hint of dust, of death.

"Kiss me, Richard of England," she said, against his mouth, "three times. Three times is the charm, Richard, and all the world can be yours."

Close, she smelt of a wild growing things, the grass, the flowers, the sap in the trees. The scent was overwhelming, as was her proximity, and he kissed her fiercely, no tenderness in his touch.

"Lie with me," she said. "That is my command."

He felt no desire but it was as if he had no control of his senses, or his own body. He looked at her, and suddenly she was Anne, his first lover Kate, and every other woman he had ever desired, all in one. She pulled him in against her, unfastening the silver doublet she had given him earlier. Her white hands were stroking his flesh, his right shoulder, his back.

"So...where is this deformity that causes you such grief?" she said. "I see nothing."

He glanced down at his own torso. His skin was pale, gleaming in the half-light. His rib cage, which had been uneven on his right side, thrown out of alignment by the curve in his spine, was now straight. He ran his fingers over each rib, one by one, marveling at their feel, their straightness, their symmetry. He then glanced from his right shoulder to his left...they were both the same. Identical. Perfect. Again, he could have wept but there were no tears he could cry.

"I told you I could give you everything," said the Queen smugly. "My new, perfect, beautiful knight."

She drew him down to her upon the grass, enfolding him in her embrace. Her body was like a statue, without flaw, without blemish...but cold as a statue too, frigid to the touch, moon-kissed marble in a churchyard. Despite the caresses, the embraces as her flesh slid sensuously against his, lip to lip, breast to breast, thigh to thigh, there was no true passion between them, just motions that mimicked those of life, a sorry, mocking semblance of the ancient dance between man and woman. And if it bound the sexes together in the world of the living, it was binding Richard in this half-life to something darker that he did not wish to understand...

Suddenly revolted, Richard pulled away from the Queen and flung himself on his belly in the grass, unable to bear to look at her. She sat up, and anger shone in the lamps of her eyes; they were hooded, green; their coldness reminded him of the hated Woodville woman.

"What ails you, my knight, my lover?" A hint of deadly poison spiked the lash of her voice; the bite of the serpent.

"This...*all of it*!" Wildly, he waved his arm toward the unfinished drink and food, to his fine garments strewn on the ground, and lastly, he gestured to his perfect, even shoulders. "It is not real. It is created by the 'glamour' of your unholy Fay realm. I...I am not your 'perfect knight.' You are not my lady or my mistress. You bid me lie with you but for what? You do not feel, I do not feel, I cast no seed...*I AM DEAD!*"

He bent over, bowed with grief; it was as if he had taken a physical blow. "Lift your enchantments from me and leave me be. Lost I may be, a fallen man, crooked of limb and unwholesome...but, by Christ, you will not make me your plaything...If naught else, I *WILL REMAIN RICHARD*, and go to whatever doom is my due!"

The Queen of Elfland sprang to her feet in a fury, and for a moment, he thought she would strike him. Instead, she made a wild gesture with her hands, and in the air, figures began to form, born of mist and cloud and will o' the wisps. "Foolish man, you reject my gifts and swear to remain as you were," she snapped. "See how they will remember you, Richard Plantagenet, and then tell me that what I offered you, the balm of dreams, the sweetness of the unreal, was not preferable!"

A dreadful and poignant scene appeared before Richard's gaze. His own corpse displayed in the Church of the Annunciation in Leicester's Newarke, naked save for a simple black cloth across his hips. On the nearby altar, mounted on a stand of gold, stood a holy relic, a thorn of the Crown of Christ...horribly poignant in the symbolism of Christ's triumphant return and Richard's ignominious one.

Crowds gathered, staring at what they never thought to see, the slain body of an anointed king, bloody and near-naked. Some wept quietly, others, eager to please their new Tudor master, jeered and spat. Then, on the third day, he was rolled onto a bier and carried under the great Newarke gate to the church of the Greyfriars, where the Franciscans hastily dug a hole too short for Richard's body and thrust the corpse in, head propped roughly up, still-tied hands slumped against his hip. Swigging from wineskins, Tudor's impatient soldiers watched the disrespectful burial and told the monks to hurry it up.

Just when Richard thought he could bear to watch no longer, this agonizing scene jolted and blurred. Time seemed to have shifted once more, and he could see a cheap marble effigy above the pit that held his mortal remains, a tomb that was mutilated and left to decay in the open air as the friary fell into dereliction. Weeds sprang across the tomb, the strangling ivy, the green moss, and then even the weathered stones were gone, smashed up or carted away for building, the memorial to the slain king lost forever in time.

He was silent, feeling as desolate as the scene. "They will not only lose your grave but that of Anne and of your Edward," said the Queen of Elfland. "But that is not the only indignity you will suffer. You will be famous, not forgotten…but you might wish you were. *Look*!"

She waved her pale hand again, and the air crackled. Out of a haze of darkness limped a figure, seemingly alone on a great wide stage. It capered, hump-backed, puffed like a toad or crouched like a springing spider. A wizened arm was clasped against its chest; one leg dragged. Clad in black velvet like to Richard's own finery, this unwholesome man old enough to be Richard's father cackled out a litany of crimes—the slaying of Prince Edward of Lancaster; the murder by drowning in malmsey of Clarence; Anne succumbing to poison by his order, the smothering of the Edward's young sons by his own hand….

Now Richard grew angry. "What foul mummery is this?" he cried, rounding on the Queen of Elfland. "How dare they mock me in this manner? If my body is not perfect, it is not as foul and wretched as that, a thing to be jeered at and belittled in some mummer's play! My sword arm is strong, my legs are strong. I am…was…a soldier of renown for all that I am small of build. Anne never loved Lancaster, nor did I slay him, though I would have gladly done so for Anne and in revenge for Queen Margaret's murder of *my* brother Edmund! Lancaster died in the rout at Tewkesbury, as all honest men know. And George…I loved George for all his folly! I was the one who reconciled him to the cause of York, and when his tongue became too free and he was arrested, I begged Edward to let him live for the blood we shared, but the execution went ahead nonetheless—the bloody Woodvilles pushed for his death. And Anne! God, we were wed for more than ten years, I would have no more harmed her than thrust my dagger into my own heart; I had her crowned with me, at my side, because I honoured her so much, my beloved consort. Yes, when the physics told me she was dying, the consumption eating her lungs, I had to think of swift remarriage, of begetting an heir, for I had no son, my boy had died…."

He suddenly choked to silence, his fists clenched, turning away from the haughty-faced faced Queen as the memories gripped him.

"And the princes…what of the princes in the tower?" she needled him, drawing close, her pale unbound hair whipping around him, scoring his face as a chill wind blew. "What of your brother's sons, whom you displaced?"

"My greatest shame…" He hung his head. "Though they were in truth bastards through my brother's lechery, I will bear that shame for eternity."

"Yes, yes," she said. "Guilty, Richard. Guilty through time, whether they died by your hand or your order or not."

"You know nothing of it." His voice was bleak.

"Maybe this is your quest then, Richard Plantagenet. To expiate that guilt, even if only within yourself."

"Maybe," he said, but there was a dull heaviness inside him. Hated, hateful….lost to heaven, but too good for hell. How could he ever expunge such guilt?

"Go then, you who turned down the chance at being the lover of the Queen of faerie, leaving behind the human world and its cruel calumnies for sweet forgetfulness." She gathered her diaphanous robes around her, and suddenly she looked ancient, robbed of beauty, robbed of youth, a hag whose face was half a skull...like the Washer at the Ford in Leicester, who had prophesied that his head would strike Bow Bridge upon his return from battle.

"Go, Richard of England. Find your way to peace and redemption if you can, for my offer will not be extended to you again!"

He turned away, eager to leave this unpredictable and unholy creature behind him. He had donned the clothes the Queen had given him, but now they were rags as poor as a beggar's, hanging in grey tatters on his frame. Out on the vast twilit plain, he saw the three roads appear again through rising mist and fog—the narrow, nigh-impassable lane with its thorny growths, the broad highway that descended to Hell, the spiral-path that wound deeper and deeper into the heart of capricious Elfland. With heavy steps, he headed toward the one that he hoped would eventually carry him, through many travails, to Heaven...if he could ever atone for the evils he had done.

As he walked along the length of the track, briars snarling round his ankles and tearing into flesh that could not bleed, he did not hear the Queen of Elfland whisper, her mordant voice mingling with the wind: "Yes, most hated of kings...but most loved too. Richard third of that name, last flowering of the White Rose. *Sinner, sufferer, scapegoat... and sacrifice!*"

Richard journeyed on and the foliage bursting through the path grew deeper, thick as a forest. Rocks and jagged stones lurched from the earth, edges sharp as sword blades. He could not tire as living men tired, but a heaviness washed over him, a kind of leeching despair, and eventually he left the trackway altogether and wandered aimlessly across the vast plain that stretched before him, pale under the sky that both changed and yet stayed eternally twilight, and had no moon, nor stars, nor trace of any sun.

After a while, he saw a circular structure looming out of the twilight, its arches dark and gaunt against the sky. It was the first sign of any building he had seen in the Middle Kingdom, and he forced his heavy limbs to carry him in its direction.

As he drew closer, he realised with a jolt that he recognized it from his former life. Memories rushed over him, a tormented jumble. Buckingham's rebellion in 1483; October storms and the Severn flooding, washing the bridges away. The Duke's men deserting him and John Morton, the serpent who had whispered treason in Buckingham's ear, fleeing the country and leaving Buckingham to be turned in by one of his own supporters. The captured Duke had been transported to Salisbury for execution, and Richard, making his way toward the cathedral town, found himself crossing a great plain, lonely and windswept, home only to the ancient dead who lay in scores of mounds scattered across the green rises. At the edge of this plain, near the coils of the Avon, on lands owned by the nuns of Amesbury priory, where Richard's distant ancestress, Eleanor of Provence, lay buried within the church, a great pagan edifice had risen in ruinous splendour, stern as death itself, doorways upon doorways, stone gallows on which time hung, suspended.

He knew it from the writings of Geoffrey of Monmouth whose book, 'History of the Kings of Britain,' he owned and treasured—*Chorea Gigantum*, the Giant's Dance, Stonehenge of the Hanging Stones, said to have been wrought by the wizard Merlin to commemorate the fallen men of the great Roman commander, Ambrosius Aurelianus.

He had lingered there awhile in the centre of the circle, in a brief respite from all his troubles, staring up at wide skies filled with storm-clouds and skylarks, and pondering on time and death and destiny, on how the mightiest king and the greatest edifice built by man can be overthrown…by time if not by sword.

In a melancholy mood, he had then ridden on past Amesbury to Old Sarum and then Salisbury, where Buckingham awaited his fate confined within the attic room of the Blue Boar inn on the Market Place. None knew the pain Richard felt, to do his duty and execute the rebel who had been false friend. False in so many ways that none but Richard knew of, and of which he dared not tell...for who now would believe?

Buckingham... *Most untrue creature living...*

Richard stepped forward, gaze scanning the structure before him, the Giant's Dance of the Middle Kingdom. It was the same monument he had visited near Amesbury and yet different.

Here, in this tricksy, unreal world, the temple was not ruinous as in the world of living men, but stood complete as it had in ancient times. An unbroken ring of lintels spanned the tops of the outer circle, and inside loomed an army of smaller stones, vaguely human of aspect and vaguely sinister, as if they were possessed of malignant spirits that longed to emerge from their stone casings. Five freestanding trilithons, the stone gallows, towered over the rest of the monument, the one in the south-west being the tallest of all, and trails of green, noxious phosphorescence swirled through its archway and were drawn into the western sky.

He thought he could see faces trapped in that mist, some fair and sorrowful, full of longing and pity, others cruel and unforgiving, mocking him as he watched.

A peel of laughter made him jump. A child's laughter...no, children. Children playing. An ominous sensation enveloped him, and he took a tentative, unwilling step into the great circle. Bones crunched beneath his feet; he could see a cranium, small, infant-sized, and a mountain of finger bones, teeth, the detritus of the ancient dead. Dead like him...how long ago was it now?

A flash of gold caught his eye and he whirled on his heel, the bones crumbling beneath his feet. Between the arches of the stones, running in and out, in and out with childish abandon, were two young blond-haired boys. He knew those boys, knew them well. His brother's sons, Edward and Richard, whose birthright had been lost due to Edward's licentiousness, his lusts blotting out his good sense...though some men claimed Edward's bigamous marriage to Eleanor

Talbot was a web of lies Richard contrived with Bishop Stillington in order to wrest the crown from young Edward.

He shook his head wearily. Who would not think his brother the type of man to gull a woman into bed by promises of marriage? Edward, for all that Richard had loved him in his youth, was notorious; he had married the Woodville witch on May 1, day of false Greenwood weddings, and doubtless would have left her like Eleanor Talbot, if her huge, meddlesome family had not become involved.

Watching the children play, great pain filled Richard as he noted the likeness to Edward in their features and mannerisms. Their hair was a lighter hue than their father's, a spun-gold from the Woodville side, but they had Ned's easy smile, his demeanor; and both promised to be tall in manhood.

The boys chased each other, whirling around the standing stones, and Richard followed them, though they seemed to be unaware of his presence. *Amends*...He wanted to make amends, but how could he atone for the terrible evil that had befallen them? It was too late. *Far too late*.

The boys ran around again, their laughter bouncing off the stony faces of the great grey monoliths. They danced a fairy circle round Richard and then, suddenly and unexpectedly, one of them threw a stone. It skittered in the bone-dust at Richard's feet, and with a jolt, he realized that the boys had changed. No longer were they the happy little lads, so much like Ned, playing innocently amidst the stones. Now they were jeering and sneering Woodville brats with narrowed eyes and mouths quirked into smirks.

Young Edward glowered at him with disgust; a weak-chinned creature with yellowish hair and eyes underscored by circles. "Uncle, what are you doing here?" he asked in an imperious voice. "Are you dead like us? You're not king here. I will be king and you will be bones...like these..." He kicked petulantly at the twig-like heaps on the ground, making them disintegrate into a white spray.

"Forgive me," said Richard hoarsely, although, seeing these transformed children with their hard, changed, goblinish faces, he suddenly, guiltily, realised he did not truly like them or mourn them at all, Edward's sons or no.

As he stared at the transformed children, their hostility almost palpable, he sensed another presence enter the great circle, passing through the northern archway. He shuddered; legend had it that the Devil dwelt in the north; that is why all churches had a north door, the Devil's door, to let the evil one out. But this devil approaching had a certain familiarity, and a terrible one. Someone he thought he would never see again on earth or in Heaven...though Hell would have been a likelier meeting place.

Slowly he turned around; tense and strained, wishing he had a weapon to hand, though he knew not if it would be useful in these glamour-tainted lands where the dead yet lived and the sun never shone.

Harry, Duke of Buckingham stood before him, lounging against one of the smaller standing stones. He was wearing his finest garments, crimson silk the hue of blood, an orange plume on his hat, and cloth of gold he was not entitled to wear, royal ancestry or no. His face was pale, bloodless, the lips blue, rotten. Curling hair clung to his brow, bleached of colour, almost like cobwebs. His head was on his shoulders; a most extraordinary thing...for in Salisbury's Market Square, the executioner had headed Buckingham with one skilled blow, then placed his head in a woven basket and sent it to the house by the cathedral where Richard had lodged while the traitor met his end.

"Take it away, goddamn you, and give him a decent burial!" the King had snarled at the men who brought the basket as proof that the execution had been duly carried out. He could see blood dripping through the wickerwork, could smell its iron tang, and it sickened him to the core.

Buckingham...who had once been his friend, his supporter, riding with him to Northampton after Edward the King had died. Urging him all through the night in a Northampton inn not to be a fool, not to trust Anthony Woodville, to arrest him before Woodville used his greater forces to kill them both. Harry Stafford, who had spoken eloquently before the people on London, convincing them of Richard's rightful entitlement to the throne. Harry, who had done *something,* something terrible, before he suddenly turned traitor and raised a rebellion in the west. He had begged to see Richard at the end, claiming he had important information that he must hear....Richard had refused. He did not want to see that face again. Ever.

Now here it was, in this cruel Afterlife, floating like a cold, mocking moon before his repulsed gaze.

"No greeting, cousin?" The Duke of Buckingham's brows lifted and he held out his arms for an embrace. He took a step forward and at this distance, Richard could see a thin, red, crusted line across his throat and a smear of blood at the corner of his lips. "Will you not kiss me in welcome?"

"Get away from me, Harry!" warned Richard. "Or I will see you dead a second time!"

Buckingham laughed; almost a mad giggle. "Richard, dear Richard, we are all equals here, beyond the laws and mores of mortal men. There is no need for more hostility between us."

"Is there not?" said Richard fiercely. "I know what you did, Harry Buckingham! You doomed us both."

"I did it for you, cousin." Buckingham shrugged. "It is not as if you hadn't thought of it. You had to think of it. You are as guilty as I am."

"Did it for me?" Richard exploded in rage. "When did you ever do anything but for yourself, Harry? What was your real aim...the throne?"

"But of course," grinned Buckingham. "And why not? It was indecently easy to put you there. Why not me instead? I would have been content to stand behind you, a Kingmaker like unto Warwick, the power behind the throne...but you did not give me enough, Richard, never enough."

"What more could I have given you? You were the most powerful man in the land after me! You were High Constable...I made sure you got back the Bohun lands you craved so much!"

"So blind..." Buckingham sighed and he shrugged. "You were never a good judge of character, cousin. Do you not remember when you slighted me? No? One night, before your progress, I put it to you that your son should marry my daughter. It would have been a fitting match—we are both of royal blood—and it would have united our houses. You hardly even glanced up from the papers you were signing. "Impossible, Harry," you mumbled at me, as if I were some stupid serf. "Edward must marry a foreign princess to make an alliance." You shamed me, and my heart turned against you. Why should I not have been King in your stead? John Morton convinced me it could be so…though he was a liar, like so many churchmen."

"You were wrong…so wrong…I never sought to shame you; I trusted you. Until you did the most awful deed and thought that I would be grateful for it! How I loathe you, Harry."

"And now we are both dead and trapped in this purgatory," said Buckingham, almost cheerfully. "I suppose it could be worse…we might be in Hell!"

"Being here with you, it is like Hell!" Richard backed away from his treacherous cousin. Above the great stones, thunder rumbled. Clouds that glowed yellow, full of unleashed fury, peppered the dome of the sky. Wind rose, screeched, whistling between the arches of the circle. Dust eddied, rising in whirlwinds.

The two young princes ceased playing between the monoliths and stood still as stones themselves, listening as they gazed into the north. Their countenances had lost the hard maliciousness that Richard had briefly seen and they were Ned's boys again, innocent and fearful as the clouds tiered, spiraling up like sorcerer's towers, and lightening slashed down over the distant hills. "She is coming," whispered young Richard, tremulous. "Coming from her cave. We should hide, brother."

Edward grasped his brother's pale white fingers. "We must run. We are not safe here; there is no one to protect us, just as there was no one in our old life in the world of men. Especially not the Lord Protector." He shot Richard a withering, contemptuous glare, once again the look of a Woodville about him.

Hand in hand, the boys darted from the circle and scurried like frightened hares toward a nearby clump of the rancid-scented May trees that grew in that land. Their golden heads bobbed like two suns in the growing darkness; their velvet doublets were speckled rain and with leaves blown on the gale.

"What is it, what is coming?" Richard strode after them, squinting into the howling wind. "I will help you. I swear it...I will protect you from whatever you fear! Tell me what is wrong!"

The princes kept on running without a backwards glance. They vanished into the May Trees, which were bending double in the storm. White blossom fountained up and foamed about like sea froth.

"Too late," said Harry Buckingham softly, an evil little smile on his lips. "As ever, cousin."

A peal of overhead thunder blasted the Giant's Dance, making the standing stones tremble from the tops of their lintels to their bases buried deep in the enchanted soil below. Hail pummeled down, bouncing balls of ice that would have stung had Richard been able to feel pain. From the distant hills a curling, coiling funnel swept along, crowned by the lightning, tearing up earth and trees and stones in its wake. The roar of it was terrible, the sound of the very earth in agony as soil was rent and boulders broken and roots torn.

"She's in there, riding the storm, and she will get what she desires," said Buckingham, watching with cold, dispassionate eyes as the unnatural tornado swept toward the stone circle. It veered at the last minute, as if fearing something within that mighty structure, and then enveloped the stand of May-trees where the two young princes had hidden. "She always gets her prey."

"She? Who is she? What is she? " Wind-battered, Richard clung to a stone, scarcely able to stay on his feet. He tried to move forward, but the force of the storm was too strong.

"Black Annis." Harry Stafford's voice was terse. "That's what they call her here. A hag...who eats children. She lives in a hilltop cavern where she dresses in the skins of her victims. " He smirked. "I have met her like in my old life too, cousin, oh yes... Ah, what a lesson learned; it is not necessarily the whore with welcoming thighs that is a man's ruin. It can be the pious, saintly dame who is full of guile for her own ends…she also devours her victims."

The hair stood up on the back of Richard's neck. When he was a child, one of his nurses at Fotheringhay had been a woman from a Leicestershire village. To make him and George behave when they were more inclined to play than study, old Joan Booker would fill their heads with tales of a terrible hag who feasted on naughty, inattentive children. She had both boys shaking under the covers of their beds, afraid of every tap of the wind on the shutters, until Dame Cecily found out and dismissed Joan curtly: "*I will not have my sons' heads filled up with superstitious peasant nonsense!*"

Richard had quickly forgotten the old legend, its horrors leaving his mind with the passage from childhood to adulthood but now, everything had changed. Could Joan's legend be true, in this land set between Heaven and Hell? Yes, *anything* could be true here; he had witnessed that many times already. He remembered Agnes Black, the crone upon Bow Bridge, predicting his head would strike the bridge-side when he returned from Bosworth. Was that raving old woman the earth-bound copy of the monstrous witch of this land?

The twisted clouds that had heralded the arrival of Black Annis abruptly departed, receding with unnatural speed toward the shadowy hills on the distant horizon, a line of giant's heads slumbering in the surreal twilight of the Middle Kingdom. The trees where the princes had taken refuge from the witch lay strewn across the ground, their roots poking skyward and their boughs stripped bare by the force of her fury. There were no children anywhere in sight, just a small strip of blue velvet caught on one skeletal tree-branch. It fluttered, a pathetic flag.

"She has them," said Buckingham, almost gloating. "She has what she wanted."

"I must go after them," said Richard grimly.

"Noble, tragic Richard, seeking to wash the slate clean," Buckingham mocked, his grin unpleasant. "Do you think you can atone? Do you? What about me? And Rivers and Grey? Hastings. You will dwell here forever, trying to expiate your sins—face it. Here with me, your loving cousin, for eternity…"

He reached out, his hand cold, grey, claw-like. In horror, Richard struck at it, the mottled corpse's hand that groped for his wrist. "Be gone from me, you fiend of the devil!" he cried. "I had enough of you in life!"

A high, shrill peel of malevolent laughter echoed around the stone circle, and ball lightning bounced off the top of the lintels. Buckingham's ghost vanished, but not before maliciously whispering into Richard's ear the words of Harry's personal motto, *"Souvente Me Souvene*…Remember me Often."

In the hellish revenant's place, an adder coiled, puffed up to strike—Richard grabbed a storm-broken branch and struck at it and the serpent hissed and slithered away into the grass.

Richard sprinted from the Giant's Dance and out into the open plains, hurrying toward the distant hills where the clouds always boiled, a shroud of darkness that hid God only knew what. He did not know if the children he sought to rescue were truly his brother's sons, or merely beings of faerie glamour sent by the Queen of Elfland to torment him, but he also knew, somehow, that he could not turn away and leave them to their fate. Not this time. Whoever, whatever they were, he would see that they came to no harm. A pointless quest it might be, but it was *his* quest, a balm for soul and conscience.

After what seemed a journey of many days, trudging along rutted paths where the supernatural storm had left the ground rent like the belly of a man ripped open by a blade, the lonely plain came to an abrupt end. The hills towered over Richard, bald, dark mounds, treeless and blasted as if lightning had scorched them many times, killing all verdant growth on their surfaces. Cold, serpentine rivers curved around their feet, mirroring the starless sky and churning over fangs of rocks that thrust out of the water—the teeth of an angry and hostile earth.

Richard's gaze was drawn upwards, toward the hilltops. Clouds weltered upon them, bursting with black rain that skirled through streambeds like blood pouring down the gully of a sword. Carrion crows wheeled about the mouth of a cavern that opened in the side of the broadest hill, surmounted by capstones of iron-stained granite that dwarfed even the stones of the Giant's Dance. More crows sat squabbling on the branches of a lightning-blasted oak that guarded the entrance to the cavern, their raucous caws redolent of death and despair. An air of desolation hung across the entire landscape, while a sullen, foul smoke that held the essence of the pyre drifted from the edifice upon the bald hill.

Richard wished he had a weapon. He felt naked, helpless, even though he no longer had to fear death, for death had found him already. Dead though he might be, however, he had no illusions that he was invincible, and he suspected Black Annis, female or not, was far more powerful than he.

Restively he began to pace the river bank, searching amidst the water-rolled pebbles and reeds for a sharp implement or a stone light enough to carry but heavy enough to crush a skull if need be. He found nothing he could use to defend himself, and his frustration grew, knotting in his breast. Beyond the realm of men he might walk, but his Plantagenet temper still survived through death, and, uttering an oath, he stormed furiously along the river-bank, kicking at the useless stones and feeble reeds.

Suddenly he caught sight of a pillar of wind-carved quartz standing on the bank of the flowing river. The height of a man, it turned a pale stone face towards him and reflected the shimmery light of the Middle Kingdom. It seemed to beckon him forward with stern authority, as if some spirit, older than time, dwelt within its core, summoning him forward.

A jolt of suspicion ran through him; why should he feel an attracted to such a pagan object, looming in the murk like an idol of the olden times? But he felt no malice, no stink of devilish brimstone around it, and he thought of the words of Christ *'Upon this rock I will build my church, and the gates of hell shall not prevail against it.'* There was no church here, of course, in this land caught between Heaven and Hell, but perhaps he could find some consolation, something familiar, something good and pure to cling to, amidst the strangeness of his journey.

He walked around the pillar, slowly, unsure. It cast no shadow.

A sword was thrust into its flank.

He paused, staring in wonder. Such a sight...it was as if he had entered a dream. From childhood onwards, he had read and admired the legends of the great Arthur, King of the Britons; father of chivalry and nobility—what youth of rank and honour did not? The Sword in the Stone...oh yes, such a stirring tale, when the boy Arthur, alone of all the nobles in Britain, had been able to draw the blade and win the crown.

The Rightful King.

Filled with trepidation, he approached the monolith. Arrayed with tiny jewels, the sword hilt glittered temptingly. Dare he touch it? Try to draw it? Was he 'true' enough, as Arthur had been, or was he just, as some men said, the Usurper, traitor to his brother's memory, the oppressor of his progeny?

His fingers touched the hilt, closed around it. The metal felt cool but strangely comforting. He pulled, gently, then more strongly...and the sword slid from the stone as if slicing through warm butter.

But it was broken. Sheared off half way down the blade, a jagged break. Devastated, he cradled it against his chest—the broken sword, surely a symbol of his broken kingship. *A symbol of his death and dishonour.* He wrapped his hand round the stump of blade as if willing it to grow suddenly whole; it cut into his flesh, but left no mark, drew no blood...for it could not. Not anymore.

After a moment or two of shock, anger overcame him. With a cry of rage, he cast the broken sword out into the river. It spiraled through the air, gemstones flashing, and suddenly he noticed a word written across the cross-guard of the hilt.

Resurgam...I Shall Rise Again.

The sword smote the surface of the water, clove it, and descended to the depths in a stream of silver bubbles. Richard stood watching as it vanished, a sense of anticipation of sweeping over him; his body tingled, his muscles tightened; it was almost like being *alive* again. The wind seemed to drop away, sucked from the sky, and it was as if all of the Middle Kingdom paused, hushed, expectant, waiting for what would come next.

And as if in a legend from the time of the blessed Arthur, Merlin's foster-child and protégée, the sword returned from the deep, perfect and whole, reforged in that watery lair by magical arts—a beam of silver light that sheared through the water and rose, point upward to the sky, borne up from the waters by unseen hands.

On its renewed blade more words shone out, graven into the steel and burning with ice-blue flame—*Vincit qui se vincit... transit umbra, lux permanets* ...He conquers who conquers himself. Shadow passes, light remains.

Richard splashed out into the stream, drawn by the brightness, the purity of the sword that was broken, now made whole. The waters rose to his waist and higher; glancing down he could see lights where lights should never have glowed, the outline of watery temples and spires, of chalices rimmed by pearls and heroes' swords hurled into the deeps and long forgotten. He grasped the mended sword in both hands; below, he saw spectral fingers slipping from the hilt, an arm in white samite. Then the blade lay shining across his palms, lambent flame, showering droplets of water like quicksilver.

"Too good for such as me," he murmured, "I am unworthy...but I will treat it with honour, to destroy what is evil in this world and to cut away all that is false. For that I will name it, not Cut-steel, nor any other martial name—but *Veritas Lux Mea*...Truth is my Light."

He waded back out of the stream, water streaking down his legs, and bound the sword to the worn twine belt that held his pauper's rags to his body. Then he began making his way along the riverbank to the foot of the broad dark hill where the cavern of Annis gaped like a mouth into the Underworld, a vast maw that led to unknown horrors. He sent up a silent prayer and then began the ascent as storm clouds gathered, whirling in rotation over the summit of the hill.

As Richard reached the flat, rimmed top, the clouds burst like bloated corpses left on a battlefield, and lightning and hail struck the ground around him. The carrion birds screeched and took flight from the great oak, their beaks snapping as they tangled with each other in furious fight. The cave mouth gaped, lit from within by red firelight, a vision of the Hell warned of by the priests. It belched like some unholy furnace, reeking smoke pouring from within its fastness and coiling around stalactites that formed a natural portcullis across the entrance.

Warily Richard stepped under the spikes and into the stronghold of the witch Black Annis. What he saw was fouler than anything he had encountered in the deepest dungeons of Warwick or Pontefract. Heaps of skulls lay piled against the walls, rising top to bottom. Children's skulls by their small size, some very old, fringed with moss, others new, shining like pale round moons in the smoky darkness. It was almost like an ossuary, there were so many skeletal remains, but these had not been gathered together in peace and honour. They had been deliberated stacked up, gruesomely positioned in heartless warning…the leavings of millennia of feasting by the Leicestershire witch.

Richard took another step forward, drawing Truth is My Light from his makeshift belt and slinking along the passageway, careful not to disturb its grisly decoration. The cavern widened into an antechamber that consumed the heart of the hill. A roof stained with soot soared overhead, and in the centre of the flagstoned floor burned a fire-pit, its scent charnel and the flames green, fired by some unknown sorcery.

Above it, suspended on chains, like the centerpiece at some king's elaborate banquet, was the vast effigy of a tower, with grated door and adamant turrets, but made from mud, ordure, and other loathsome substances. Worms coiled from its base and crawled from narrow window-slits; yellow bile-froth trickled from the doorway and spattered on the floor.

With a start Richard realised it was an obscene, mocking version of the Tower of London, the place where all Kings spent the night before their Coronation. Inside this monstrosity, behind the iron grate, he could see the two boys who appeared to be his brother's sons, huddled together like birds before a storm. They appeared meek and wholesome again, the image of hateful Woodville brats having faded from their soot-streaked faces. They were pale as ghosts, still as statues, waiting in sad resignation.

Richard made to go to them, intent on cleaving the wall of that dark tower open with his blade, but the sound of something shuffling, dragging along the floor, forced him to retreat into the shadows, holding the sword close to prevent the firelight catching on the edge and revealing his presence. He feared nothing, in death as in the last moments of his life, but he would not risk failure of this quest through misguided bravery. He had learned that lesson one final time on Redemore...although he was subtly aware that his course had been destined, bound in the stars, although such a thing still seemed anathema to him, sacrilegious, tainted with the evils of augury and astrology.

The stench of rotting meat, sweet but rank, permeated the air, and the hag Black Annis, mother of storms, dwindled goddess of winter and death, shuffled into the chamber. Crouched and bone thin, her flesh was corpse blue, speckled with dark, necrotic blots. Ape-like arms dangled from bony shoulders, while curved talons scraped the ground, leaving long scratches in the dirt. At the waist, a grisly belt of plaited human skin girt her black, nun-like robes. Obscured by a tangle of iron-grey hair, Richard could not see her visage, but he could hear her voice as she unsheathed a flint dagger from her skin-belt, and shuffled towards the tower-prison where the two boys huddled, immobile, watching her like rabbits ensnared by the hypnotic eyes of a snake.

To Richard's surprise, Black Annis was singing a twisted version of an old cradlesong as she limped across the flagstones. She paused between each line, breaking into breathy cackles, as her claw caressed her dagger, testing the sharpness of the honed flint:

"Lavender's blue, dilly dilly,
Lavender's green

When you are king, dilly dilly,
I shall be queen
Who told you so, dilly dilly,
Who told you so?
'Twas my own heart, dilly dilly,
That told me so
Call up your friends, dilly, dilly,
We have for them work...
Collecting the taxes, dilly dilly,
With good Morton's Fork.
Lavender's blue, dilly dilly,
Lavender's green
When my son is king, dilly dilly,
I shall be queen!"

A strange uneasiness gnawed at Richard as he heard the witch sing out the name of John Morton, his long-time enemy and conspirator with Buckingham in his failed rebellion. The refrain of '*I shall be Queen!*' also alarmed him. He was reminded uncomfortably of a woman he had known, pious to madness, her prayers filled only with entreaties for herself and her cursed family. A woman who had plotted against him, ostensibly to free Edward's sons from the Tower, but who naturally wanted her own son to sit on the throne in their place. A woman he should have executed for treason, but instead delivered to her husband's keeping because Richard of England did not kill women.

A woman whose son had brought his foreign rabble to England's shores to kill an anointed king.

With a cry of anguish at the memory, Richard sprang from his hiding place, Truth is My Light a pure flame that chased away the darkness, sending shadows spinning up the walls. Whatever it was crouched before him, singing sinister childhood songs as it sloped towards the Tower with dagger in hand, it had to be banished to whatever Hell it had come from.

Sensing his presence, Black Annis whirled to face him with terrifying speed, howling like the storms she raised. The face beneath the tangled knots of hair, though blue-black as death and filled with teeth of iron, was the prim, gaunt visage of

Henry Tudor's mother, chaste wife of Lord Stanley—Margaret Beaufort.

Richard halted with the shock of that encounter, although it had been half-expected after hearing the telling words in the witch's murderous lullaby. Annis's venomous eyes raked over him, bird-bright, a carrion crow's hungry gaze. She licked her lips and opened her mouth, and blew forth a foul gobbet of flies that buzzed around Richard as if he were meat for them to devour.

At the same time, his sword arm felt weak and withered, as if its strength had been sapped. Once before, on that dreadful day when he had ordered Lord Hastings' execution after receiving intelligence that Hastings had brought hidden weapons to destroy him, he suffered a similar malady... his sword arm weak and tingling, his breath shallow and uneasy in his lungs, a sensation of impending doom hanging over him. He had suspected witchcraft then, and he knew beyond a doubt that it was in use now.

"You were a fool," Annis spat. "Noble, loyal Richard with his band of gauche northerners who did everything wrong...and now history will hate you for it. To think, you let me carry Anne's train at the Coronation! I could have spat upon it. But in the end I got my revenge, I got the honour due me—I sign my name 'Margaret Regina' when it pleases me. I had your prayer book for my own, you know, after my son rifled your tent, and lovely it is too. I tried to erase your name from the pages but alas, it is still there...."

She smirked at him, a horrible grimace, the iron tips of her teeth glinting beneath her lips. "I have won, and you have lost. You will be trapped here in purgatory forever, too evil and hated to ever ascend to Heaven—even God turns from you—but, for whatever reason spared the fires and turning spits of Hell."

"No..." he breathed, shaking his head. The tip of his sword dropped down; the hilt almost twisted from his numb, tingling hand. The idea of remaining in the Middle Kingdom forever, in a land of demented fantasy where he had no friends, no loved ones, nothing but treacherous ghosts like those of Buckingham to torment him, was unbearable beyond anything he could imagine. He would almost prefer Hell, because at least one could not hold to false hope in its burning pits. "I do not believe you; your words always twisted the truth to suit your own ends..."

With an effort, he raised Truth is My Light again, though his fingers shook with the strain; it was as if an unseen assailant was trying to push his arm down, to disarm him before this malign creature of deceit and winter's cold.

Black Annis raised her claws to her face as if to protect herself from a blow, but she peered coyly, smugly, between the honed nails, each as sharp as a dagger-blade.

"You wouldn't harm me, would you?" she wheedled. "You don't harm, women, Richard Plantagenet, that is well known. You did not kill me despite my plotting against you; you merely released me to my husband who laughed at your softness. You did not kill Jane Shore, that simpering harlot who bedded Hastings and Thomas Grey as well as your brother, and ruined Edward's health by encouraging his dissolute ways. She spied for your enemies as well as spread her legs for them, and still you spared her. You were also kind to Edward's daughters, all of whom could have contested you for the throne, since England does not have Salic law like France..."

"Say no more," his voice was soft in the shadowy vault. "You are right...I do not kill women. Even now." He suddenly slammed the point of Truth against the ground and leaned forward on the blade, as if all fight had left him. His head was bowed, his chestnut hair falling over his face like a shroud.

In the back of the cave, the two boys who bore the visages of Edward's sons regarded him in silence. Their cheeks were marble, their eyes black coals. Watching, watching...judging.

Black Annis lifted her flint dagger, its edge winking in the gloom, and suddenly she proffered it to Richard hilt-first. "This blade is named Desolation," she hissed. "Take it...my only gift to one such as you, the consolation prize for the loser of both throne and life, of hope and faith. Use it upon yourself, and the torment of this half-life will end for you forever. There will be nothing more for you, save old bones mouldering in a grave lost to men. No purgatory...no Heaven...no Hell, no hope of salvation, no chance of damnation. Just...nothing...just the unending, quiet dark. Forever."

Richard glanced at the deadly stone blade. To end this wretched existence, to lie quiet and unknowing until the end of Time. Was such an end preferable to seeking for what might never be? Had his faith been ill-spent, were his sins too great for redemption? He almost reached out, his fingers trembling, seeking the release, the darkness, the end of all suffering...

But...surely to commit such an act, to cast his own spirit into darkness, was a sin, even if his mortal life was already gone?

God help me, show me the way; I am so lost and seek the Light....

He could not do it. No matter his despair, he would not follow the dark path that went against all he had ever believed in, in life or death. He recoiled from the proffered knife, a new resolve boiling up inside him. His lost strength returned; his could feel his arm, his fingers. He would not take the coward's way out of the Middle Kingdom; would not fall to the temptations of the creature that bore the face of his enemy.

He swung up Truth is My Light, which clove the air with an exultant shriek. "I reject the doom you offer, witch! And yes, it is true... I do not kill women. But you are not a woman and you are not, in truth, Margaret Beaufort, no matter how conniving that dame was during my life. You are a demon sent to torment me, to try me, and so you will perish, along with all other false visions in this cave."

The sword slashed down, rays of luminescence beaming from the writing on the blade *'shadow passes, light remains...'* The shoulder of the witch was struck a mighty blow and Black Annis shrieked, smoke and fire belching from her mouth as she writhed in agony. Cold-fleshed was the witch, the harbinger of winter, but in the bag of her distended belly flames burned as in a foul oven, and now they burst forth, dragon-hot. Her iron teeth began to melt, dripping down her face like molten icicles.

Flames surged about Richard and he felt an unexpected searing sensation on his skin, but he was past caring. If this should be his end, it was in good fight against this vile creature of darkness, this deceiver. He swung Truth is My Light again, and it severed the hag's ribcage and plunged down through her body, striking against the floor of the cave, where it shattered against the flagstones. Serrated fragments flew through the air, spiraling balls of light that tore through the gloom of the cavern.

A violent wind screeched into the witch's stronghold, carrying Black Annis's dying screams upon its breath. The tempest forced Richard to his knees, amidst sparkling shards of metal and witch-blood that burned into the rocks like acid. The skulls heaped at the cave mouth were hurled about in the whirlwind, bouncing off the walls like grisly balls before being sucked away, out of the grotto into the lowering sky beyond. The clay Tower where the princes were imprisoned broke free of the chains from which it hung suspended and crashed to the ground, turning over on its side. Its turrets buckled and broke and the mud-washed walls cracked, spewing flames that quickly encircled the whole construction, burning and consuming.

Richard sprang towards it, clawing his way along the floor in the deadly wind, but the heat of the flames and the whirlwind beat him back and he ended up crouched before the wreckage, helpless with fear and rage.

Suddenly the grating on the fallen prison burst open with a clang, and two white birds flew out and dived for the cave-mouth, avoiding the flames that leaped and flickered to touch the ceiling. Birds white as new snow, pure as untouched souls. They soared toward the east at great speed, wings flashing against the sullen purple of the heavens, seeking freedom beyond the circles of the world, leaving within their shattered prison no signs of children, living or dead, nor any other creature. Whatever, whoever they were, they had left behind what they once were and would never return; their purpose complete, their destiny fulfilled.

Black Annis let out one final, wrenching wail and her talons stretched out after them, fingers of darkness and smoke curling toward the empty eastern sky, but she was too late… Her riven body collapsed in a heap, and turned to ash that the gale scattered throughout the chamber.

The wind ceased to scream and a sudden calm fell.

Richard was alone. No hag. No princes. No one.

The fire in the centre of the cave flickered out, and on the cavern's mighty capstone, a cleansing rain began to patter, dripping through cracks like so many spilled tears. He cradled the ruins of Truth is My Light in his arms and knelt on the floor, his position one of a man deep in prayer.

Yet he did not pray, for no words would come to him in this place of great evil and yet of great victory—over Black Annis, over his own human frailty and weakness. It was a place of letting go of what was past, of obtaining freedom from his own doubts, the chains of bitter memory that bound him ….just as the white birds, whatever they truly were, had found freedom in the skies, upon the wind, away from all towers, all prisons.

Away from Death itself.

A sense of peace and quietude fell over him, such as he thought he would never experience again, if his existence lingered on until Judgment Day. If it was not contentment, it was acceptance. For the first time since he had entered the Middle Kingdom, his lips formed the faintest arc of a smile.

Chapter Six—THE KING IN THE CARPARK

Richard remained for an untold time within the witch's cavern high upon the enchanted hills of the Middle Kingdom. No more visions troubled him, nor did beings fair or foul disturb his peace; he was completely alone. He began to resume some semblance of life, although he was in death, his earthly body laid in a too small grave by the terrified Franciscan friars of Leicester.

On his knees, with the hilt of Truth is My Light held before him as a crucifix, he reflected on the days of his lost life and no longer begged to leave this place of purgatory. It would be done, when it was done…if such release was ever granted him.

He became as a holy monk from the early ages of Christianity, living alone in contemplation in a remote cell—following the lifestyle of his favourite saints, Ninian, who had converted the Picts and Britons in the North, and blessed Cuthbert, whose goodness was such that his body remained incorrupt after his death on the stark, windswept Farne Islands. Richard and Anne had visited Cuthbert's shrine at Durham many times and even been received into the monks' confraternity, such was their reverence for that ancient, holy man.

But Richard's newfound peace and acceptance of his confinement in the Middle Kingdom was not to last. While in his reflections of past and future, he suddenly became aware of a fissure within the quartz crystal embedded in the pommel of Truth is My Light, just above the gems that spelled the word *Resurgam*. The crack had not existed before; gazing into its fractured heart, as if into a broken mirror, he saw images flying past that broke his heart and spirit anew, and shattered the hard-bought serenity he had so recently found.

Gazing down through this glass darkly, he beheld what he guessed was the world of the living. The modern world.

A world that had long left Richard Plantagenet behind.

He saw his grave in Greyfriars, as he had seen it once before through the sorcery of the Queen of Elfland. The Friary was in ruins, abandoned and derelict, the broken arches of the roofless chancel raised to the sky like wasted bones. Ivy sprang about his effigy and weeds burst through the base of the tomb, nature claiming both bones and memorial.

But the vision did not end there, with the fall of Greyfriars. Even that sad spectacle was swept away by time; now where his bones lay there was only wasteland rank with tangled grass, and a pillar in a rich man's garden...before that too was toppled and dragged away to be smashed up and used in building works. Red brick came next, stark, unlovely buildings with windows reminiscent of sightless eyes, and a pavement covered all, locking the Friary's secrets and a long-dead King deep beneath an umbrageous blanket.

That was not all. He saw his castles in ruin; the gaunt shells of Middleham and Sheriff Hutton, Barnard and Penrith, standing broken under the cold northern skies, with birds nesting in their towers and winds singing a dirge through the empty windows he had once enlarged so that he and Anne could watch the soft play of the summer light over moor and field and town... Nottingham, his Castle of Care, had been blown up in some conflict and a house raised on the site, an ugly squat eyesore of a palace; his lavish tower, fitted out so lovingly for his comfort, had been razed to near ground level and flowers danced around its stones in manicured beds.

Grief shook him, seized him with cruel, rending talons. He saw books on shelves; the tome written by the man called William Shakespeare—and saw the caricature this writer had devised, the limping monster of the stage with his bunched back and withered arm. He saw schoolchildren at their desks learning the names of all the Kings of England in rhyme. 'Dick the Bad' was what they called him.

Dick the Bad.

Anger erupted in him, a sense of injustice wrenching his beatless heart. Whatever he had done, and by God he knew he was a man of many sins and failings, hence his plans to build a chantry for a hundred priests in York, who would pray continuously for his soul, but why was he singled out for such venom, throughout all the long years of his death? Was he truly so much worse than any other King? Than any other man?

Down through the fissure in the broken quartz he sent his burning thought into the waking world, the world lost to him untold years before on the field of Redemore, that men now called Bosworth for the nearby village of Market Bosworth.

I beg you, whoever can hearken to me...Remember me...remember me...but not as you may have heard, not as this Shakespeare claims, nor those who licked the boots of Tydder for their advancement. There is more to my story....I lived, I loved, I suffered. I did wrong....but I was a man, not some monster....I was a man...

And in the new world of cynicism, of growing disbelief and rationality, where people had begun to question old accounts and tired tropes...someone heard...someone felt...*something.*

A whisper in the dark. A vague touch on the arm while visiting an old castle. A vivid dream more real than reality. A vague scent of costmary, frankincense, a face half-remembered.

Some were afraid, confused. Some rose to the challenge, like warrior-knights of Richard's own retinue. Some wept with a grief they could not understand and thought they were going mad. Some loved beyond reason and did not question.

There was a little change in the unyielding fabric of the world...

King Richard, the last Plantagenet, was remembered with affection by those who never knew him, and the web of lies and half-truths that had been spun over untold years began slowly, very slowly to unravel...

Time stretched on, but Richard could not say how much time. He suspected it might be hundreds of years since he had fallen on Redemore, but it was impossible to gauge time with any accuracy in this twilit world of Elfland, with no planets to move across the sky to mark the passage of the days and nights. He felt a strange weariness, almost as if he were growing thin, stretched, too many years passing as he tried to restore what possibly could not be restored. Although he had touched the consciousness of many mortals on the earth and roused those who defended him as if they were his own brave knights reborn, he was still denied a final rest, a release from this purgatory imposed upon him by...the Queen of the Middle Kingdom? Or was his suffering decreed by the heavenly Father himself, who surely had precedence over that strange, fey woman, Queen or no?

It hardly mattered anymore. As ages passed, it seemed nothing he ever did would be enough to free him. Richard must do penance for eternity.

Stiffly he rose from his knees, where he had been scrying the crystal on the hilt of his broken sword. Tonight the world below, the mortal land, looked very dark, threatening; he could sense no one who was receptive to his call and it chilled him. He had seen cruel-faced and close-minded scholars mocking those who defended his name, and their scorn disturbed him, made him want to retreat from the earthly realm forever.

Perhaps there was indeed no hope, and even those he had touched would abandon him, turning back to the persuasive words of Thomas More and Shakespeare and John Rous.

Rous...Richard's lips curled in angry contempt, his fists knotting at his side. A priest at Warwick, who had written glowing words to praise Richard when he reigned as King, then, once he was dead, told the most dreadful slanders, beginning the process of making him into a monster. In the womb two years, born with sharp teeth and long hair...it was an insult to his Lady Mother, Cecily, as much as to himself. And to think, some men even in so-called enlightened modern times seemed all too eager to believe such improbable tales!

Burning with the injustice of his fate, he stalked out of the cavern into the perennial dusk of the Middle Kingdom. St Elmo's fire flickered on the remains of the dead tree that grew by the cave; the gale was up, rippling the grass and shreds of clouds tumbled in disarray across the ever-eventide sky. He scanned that endless violet expanse, changeless as the painted dome of some vast sepulchre. Never had he so wished to see the moon again; longed to see its radiance rising over

Middleham Moor, silvering the walls of his great castle as it slumbered in shadow. The castle that now lay shattered and bird-haunted, open to the snow, the rain, and the prying wind.

Tearing his gaze away from the sky, the twilit sky he had come to loathe, he suddenly caught sight of something furled in the clouds that drifted along the tops of the range of hills. He had never noticed it before, and yet he was sure he should have.

It was a mountain, a single tall peak, rising to an unknown height, its head wrapped in a heavy grey pall. He could not see the summit, only the embroiled clouds; the mountain seemed to pierce the dome of the Middle Kingdom and carry on upwards, ever upwards…maybe even reaching to Heaven itself.

It was as if a bolt of lightning had struck him. *He knew.* Whatever was there, he had to climb the mountain.

Maybe, just maybe, this final travail into the unknown would herald his escape from endless years of imprisonment with no true night and no true day, in a land where he thought as a living man and walked as a living man, yet had no blood in his veins, nor heartbeat in his chest. Maybe God finally waited for him on that high peak that had not been there a day ago, ready at last to judge his soul, to either make him pay for his earthly sins or else absolve him and grant him the peace he craved.

He hurried to the foot of the mountain and began to climb.

The way was not easy. Boulders blocked Richard's path, some wrought of hard granite, others, strewn in crooked disarray, seemingly made of deep green ice. Avalanches of shale and snow flowed past him, seeking to carry him back down the mountainside, while brambles clawed at his legs, trying to wind their way around his ankles and drag him back to the start of the path. He slashed at the vines with the shard of Truth is My Light, and they withered and turned to ash at its touch. He ploughed on, doggedly; it was his one last ambition. Nothing else mattered. He had been sundered from life for so long he hardly cared if he were to fall from the strange, surreal mountain and vanish into limbo... At least, it would be finished, a decision made at last.

After what seemed an age, the path petered out and he found himself on the edge of a narrow ravine that plunged through the mountainside, a sword-slash in its flank. Crystals and precious stones glimmered dully, revealed in that rending of the earth, while spires of dull red stone needled the sky along the lips of the crevice, clouds flicking on their tips like pennants. At the far end of this long gully, he could see a golden glow, a tracery of shining bars rising near as high as the fans of stone above him.

A gate. Tall and ornate, with bars fashioned from gleaming gold.

Could this be, here on top of the world...the Gates of Heaven?

He began to run, half-falling in eagerness as he entered the mountain cleft. The gems beneath his feet were as pebbles, worthless trinkets; he would have stepped upon his own crown and destroyed it to reach his desired goal that day...

The gate soared up before him, high and insurmountable, surely the work of God or of giants. Through the bars, he could see a fair, shining country; it was like England in a fair spring, but an England with no poverty, plague, or war....stout houses with bright beams, the village green, the reed-fringed pond, the maypole.

The Merry England Edward had tried vainly to create but failed to sustain as he succumbed to gluttony, sloth and lust.

Upon the green sward by the pond grew a broad-boled Tree, branches stretching up to embrace heaven, its leaves wrought of purest gold, its bark studded with jewels. Light flowed over its topmost boughs, forming an unearthly nimbus. Never had he seen a living thing of such beauty; its radiance banished forever the image of the twisted oak of Bestwood, with its human fruit, and the crow-haunted gallows that marked Annis's cave. Yet obliquely he knew it to be the same Tree, transformed by the all-encompassing Light, and suddenly he heard singing drifting from amidst its flowering fronds, the voices so fair surely they were those of angels:

*"It seemed to me that I gazed upon
a wonderful Tree,
lifted high in the air, wound rought with Light,
the brightest of beams.
That beacon was coated in gold;
beauteous gems stood at corners of the earth;
likewise there were five
upon the Tree's cross-beam.
Verily these were no gallows for the wicked,
but the Holy Spirit beheld it there.
Wondrous was this Victory-Tree,
and I, stained with sin,
wounded with guilt,
I saw that Tree of Glory,
covered with gold, shining with joy..."*

Grabbing the bars of the great gate, Richard tried to wrench them apart and enter this land of lost content, this England of the heart, where the Tree of Life spread over all…but the metal would not bend to his touch. With a cry, he tried again with renewed violence and, as before, failed. The bars sliced into his fingers and he stared at his hands in shock. He was bleeding, who should not be able to bleed…

Sick desperation filled him. Why had he felt driven to journey so far, only to fail, to be made a fool at the end? "I do not know what you want me to do next!" he screamed at the impassive sky.

From behind the gate, he heard a sound, his name called, soft and low. He stared, bloodied hands dropping to his sides, as Anne walked out of the strange, sweet spring, blossoms from the Tree tumbling from her unbound hair.

It was not Anne as he had seen her at the last, a wasted shell of a woman whose face already resembled the skull it would soon become. Anne, gasping for breath, her infected lungs bleeding, even as her heart bled for their loss of their son, Edward. Anne, tormented that Richard no longer shared her bed on the orders of the physicians, and by the rumours that he longed to replace her with Elizabeth of York…

No, this was Anne in the early days of their marriage, after he had rescued her from the clutches of jealous George, he an ambitious young man of about twenty, she a few years younger—Warwick's daughter, though favouring her mother Anne Beauchamp in looks rather than the swarthy Richard Neville. Practical Anne, who had always supported him, a good wife, intelligent and loyal....and he had let her down.

"Anne..." He stretched his hand to her through the bars. She took it and kissed it, paying no mind to the blood. The blood that should not have flowed.

"Oh, Dickon, Dickon, I have waited so long for you."

"Forgive me," he said, sinking to his knees.

"There is nothing to forgive. If ever there was, it was forgiven a long time ago."

"I was not as kind...as I should have been. So many times. You heard the bell ring, you thought that it tolled for you before you were even dead..."

"And you held me and kissed me and told me not to be afraid, that all would be well. Many a man would have pushed a woman away in anger if she voiced such crazed fancies, especially before an audience of evil-minded men who would whisper and make much of it. I was not thinking straight, my husband, the shadow of death clouded my mind that day."

He looked wistfully at her, hardly able to believe she was here...and that there were still barriers raised between them. "Is this Heaven, Anne, beyond this gate? Why can I not pass to be with you? Am I to be punished, to be kept away from salvation...from you...forever? Tell me, have you...have you gazed upon the face of the Almighty? Is he the stern but forgiving Lord we were told of? Would He...forgive even such a wretch as me?"

Anne's face was pale ivory, like a carving of the Madonna, radiant and calm. "It may be Heaven, Richard but I have heard it called many names here. But if it is Heaven, the lessons learned here are far different from what we were taught while on earth. And Hell...my love, there is no Hell..."

He frowned. "No Hell! But how can that be? We were always told of the punishment of the unrighteous, of the eternal flames and the demons who scourged those unrepentant of pride and murder and lust."

"My beloved Richard, I have learned that Hell is what man makes for himself in his time on earth; his doubts, his fears, his follies. And death—what is that truly? We are all…shards of light, Richard, pieces of infinity, our scraps of thought and memory falling, like stardust, to confer a bit of that which we once were to those who dwell on after us. We are in them, we move them; they are all our children. I have gazed into the face of eternity, of creation and destruction…and maybe that is truly what men name God."

"You speak like a mystic," said Richard wanly. "My mother read the work of mystics but I understand them not, and do not know if it is blasphemy or heresy. Nor, at this moment, do I care….hold me, Anne."

She pressed herself against the gate and stretched her arms through to embrace him. Their mouths met through the golden bars; he almost pulled away as he realized, in wonderment, that her mouth was not the cold, dry dustiness that he had tasted when he kissed the Queen of Elfland, but as sweet as he remembered from the days of their youth. His whole body felt almost…*alive*; he trembled at the sensations he though he would never feel again.

"What is happening to me?" he murmured, when he took his lips from hers.

"Richard, when the Queen of Elfland took you into her realm when you fell on Redemore Plain, her power over you meant you were unable to pass on into the Light as others do. You have fought valiantly to atone for all that troubles your conscience, and to free yourself from the spells of the Middle World, but alas…it is still not time. Although it pains me to say it, even after all these years you are not ready to join me yet. Not quite. The day will come when we will be united again and you may rest. But there is still much for you to accomplish…a king without a grave, a king who has lost both burial place and his reputation. There will be no peace until you are found and all is well…You must return to the living world, for a time so that this may be accomplished."

"Return!" He was shocked by her words. "That is unnatural, Anne. There is no returning from the realm of the dead, not until the Day of the Resurrection! I will not walk the modern world a sad ghost, bringing fear with me and the curses of priests."

"Not a ghost, my husband. Think of this brief span as a gift given, an exceptional case to right an old wrong...it is the message I bring to you from above. And when you have done what you must, I will be here waiting for you, for Time means nothing now, and there is no more fear of Death because there is in truth naught to fear....Our son is here too, waiting for you in the village, hale and happy, and your other children and all those you have loved. Remember the words of Luke in the Bible, Richard, if you have doubt about what you will be, for just a short time, until you have done what needs must: *"See my hands and my feet, that it is I myself. Touch me, and see. For a spirit does not have flesh and bones as you see that I have."*

"Oh Anne...I cannot believe such a thing may happen and still be righteous. Please tell me you are real, that what you say is real, and that this is not a lie of Satan sent to deceive me. I have been deceived and betrayed so many times." He leaned against the cold bars, longing to be nearer to her.

"It is no lie. It is truth, and soon you shall know it. Go in peace, my husband, until it is time for us to meet again."

Mist flooded the ravine, pouring down the gully in heavy, rolling tendrils. It rolled around Richard and Anne, obliterating the golden gates the Tree of Life, which sank into a golden haze. The higher levels of the mountain vanished into the damp coils.

"Farewell for now, Richard," said Anne, placing one last kiss to his cold cheek. Slowly she began to walk away into the mist, back toward the now-obscured Tree, the hidden village. "It is time for you to sleep, to gain strength for the final part of the battle you have fought for so long. Next time we meet, it will be for forever."

He staggered to his feet, clung to the bars willing her to return, but she was gone. Wetness streaked his face. Was it from the chill of the mist? He wiped his eyes, feeling them sting, blur...this could not be, for he was dead, a foul revenant unclean in the eyes of God and man.

He began to stumble down the mountainside, uncaring of where he placed his feet, slipping and falling on the shale and ice. Exhaustion descended on him and he almost collapsed. He was bone weary, just as he oftimes felt in life after giving battle or traveling on the long road...a different sensation to the 'stretched' lingering weariness of his imprisonment in the Middle Kingdom.

Reaching Black Annis's cavern, his hermit-cell, his sanctuary, he sank to his knees on the cold flagstones, worn and fatigued. He clutched the hilt of Truth is My Light to him, the only cross he had in this heathen Otherworld. The fissure in the crystal upon the crossguard glowed with ethereal light, stronger than he could ever recall, and he anxiously fixed his gaze upon it, wondering what it could betoken.

Images from strange worlds and times he never knew flickered hazily within the crystal's heart, drawing his very essence towards them. The pull was stronger than ever before; it was as if Time itself was unraveling, twisting and warping on some giant loom that had broken, the threads of the skein tangling before they were suddenly... *severed*....

Richard's consciousness began to fail; darkness swelled and eddied around him, a suffocating cloak pressing down, down, *down*. Against his chest, the quartz crystal in the sword-hilt fogged up, as if touched by the Breath of Life...then suddenly it shattered and its shards tumbled over him like shining tears.

The ruined sword-hilt fell from his nerveless hands, the word written upon it flashing beacon-bright in the shadows of the cavern.

Resurgam. I will rise again.

He was asleep...or was it sleep? He turned restlessly, not sure where he was or what had happened to him. Sometimes it seemed that layers upon layers of dark earth and paving rose above him, and he could hear peoples' feet echoing through the blackness, and voices raised in jest or in anger, and noises from machinery he could put no name to. Sometimes he would shift about as if seeking to rise, but he could not open his eyes to see...and he thought he could feel *'things'* in the dark, lying beside him, beneath him. Thin, brittle sticks...bones? *His bones?* He was mystified more than afraid....He was still so weary, so weary...and his thought was not clear. He was not even certain if he wanted to wake again, or just to sleep forever here in this close, strange womb.

But then...then...a rivulet of water slid into the stygian fastness that cradled him deep beneath the earth. Cold droplets trickled down and made snail's tracks across his cheek. He blinked once, twice, and then gazed up. It was dark, so dark, and he could smell damp soil and acrid fumes, bitter as wormwood. Throwing up his hands, he touched dirt and impacted rubble over his head. He was fully encapsulated, imprisoned like a man thrown into an oubliette, a bottle dungeon.

Panic gripped him...He had to get out, to escape! He knew he could not move all the heavy layers he sensed were piled over him, so he did as he had done in Annis's cavern, cast his thought, his energy, up through the shallow fissure where the rainwater had leaked in, up into the living world, seeking someone, anyone, who could sense his presence and come to his aid.

A terrific vibration tore into the lightless dome above him. He lay back, suddenly afraid of the noise, louder even than the roar of cannons, an infernal sound like the bellowing of devils in Hell. The roof of his subterranean prison began to shudder and judder; scraps of detritus showered over him. A crack appeared and a thin grey beam of light filtered into the pit, growing brighter and brighter as the crack widened, lengthened.

Daylight! How long had it been since he had seen such an ordinary but marvelous thing? He strove towards it, seeking a sun he had been denied for untold years.

The roaring stopped; he heard a gabble of voices, talking excitedly. He could not make out the words, but he did not care. *He was free!*

A mass of energy, the essence of Richard Plantagenet he burst forth unseen into the living world.

It was August 25, 2012, exactly 527 years since his body had been brought from its cruel display in the Newarke to Greyfriars in Leicester, where it was hastily dumped into a hole, without a shroud and with hands still bound.

Above the modern day car park that covered the site of the ancient friary and the king's grave, storm clouds rose from nowhere to blot the late summer sky. The heavens opened and thunder roared in mingled triumph and exultation as the most violent electrical storm seen over Leicester for many years swept in....

February 4, 2013...the month of lovers, when cards, hearts, and chocolates abound in that strange tribute to martyred St Valentine, who was beaten with stones and clubs, and then beheaded outside the Flaminian gate in Rome. A few days past the old pagan feast of Imbolc, time of lambing, first dawning of Spring, and the Christian Candlemas, which is also called Hyapante, the Meeting, in Greek.

Thousands of TV sets flicked on...an archaeological revelation was to be revealed, a once in a lifetime excavation. A great and unexpected find; the odds had been a million to one. A King lost, now found. The truth of his last mythologized hours revealed to the world; the story of his death brought to light after five hundred years by the horrifying wounds that marred his fragile, ancient bones. Legends of his remains being hurled in the River Soar by jeering mobs during the Reformation were now disproved by the evidence of the grave; many secretly reveled to find their personal suspicions correct...they had always believed he lay in Greyfriars, waiting, though how they had known so surely, they did not quite understand.

Near the end of the programme, before eagerly waiting cameras, they brought out a facial reconstruction, scientifically crafted by forensic specialists, using a cat scan of the King's war-battered skull as basis. And as the cloth covering the recon was lifted slowly, maximizing the drama of the moment, it seemed to many watching, some with only the slightest interest in the last Plantagenet King, that '*something*', an energy, shot like a bolt through the TV screen and out into the world, touching them somehow as it went by. Changing them irrevocably, as it traveled beyond and away.

The winds of a great winter storm were raging over the Isles, roaring in over the Irish Sea. Snow dusted the hills. The air was alive and the night burned with it.

Richard, last of the Plantagenets, had been given back his lost identity.

Richard, King of England, had been given back his face.

Rain slashed down, falling in vertical bands, on the modern bridge built over the long submerged foundations of Bow Bridge, where a King of England had departed to defend his crown and returned a lifeless corpse slung naked across a horse. Car headlamps gleamed through driving torrents falling from a bruised sky; raindrops pinged off the road, off the modern railings with their white and red roses.

A summer storm, significantly near the anniversary of Bosworth Field….

In Castle Park, near the slow-moving murk of the Soar and the hump of the castle motte, the trees planted as a pleasant windbreak bent almost double in the wind, their leaves tearing off in the gale and eddying like confetti around the base of a statue near the park's entrance.

It was a memorial to King Richard III, believed by some to be England's most evil monarch, a Machiavellian figure who ascended the throne in a welter of blood; others a ruler much maligned, who made good laws for the common man and who may have been considered a great king had his reign, and his life, not been cut piteously short. The statue showed the King in his final hour on the field of battle, a dagger in his right hand, his arms bare and devoid of protective armour. He held up the disputed crown to the sky, a look of anguish on his face.

At the statue's feet lay a wreath of white roses, torn by the wind, petals scattered and trodden into the pavement. A woman, wrapped in a heavy Gortex jacket, was adding a single rose...her own tribute.

She felt a little bit embarrassed, and she glanced from side to side furtively to make sure no one was watching as she placed the flower beside the tattered wreath. She had never visited Leicester before, never thought of it as any sort of tourist destination, but after seeing the TV show about Richard III's bones back in February, she had felt a strange, uncomfortable draw. It was as if she had to come here. *Had to.*

She jumped in alarm as a figure suddenly materialized from the wind and rain and blowing leaves, and joined her under the dipping tree boughs. She didn't appreciate this intrusion; she was uncomfortable enough, feeling a trifle silly, and now unsafe: a darkening, storm-tossed night, and a stranger in the park. She tried to focus on the newcomer, but his face was not clear; it was as if she gazed at him through a fragmented glass.

Damn rain, she thought, wiping at her eyes; water was dripping from her soaked fringe. *And I need my glasses....*

"Not a nice night," she said, falsely cheerful, ready to make her escape.

"No." The man's voice was slightly strange, English, but with an accent she did not immediately recognize. Touch of Yorkshire maybe...mixed with Midlands? Somehow neither. Odd. He spoke slowly, very formally, as if concentrating on his speech. "And still you brought...the White Rose."

She blushed and stared at her feet. Water was leaking into her shoes. Uncomfortable...everything was uncomfortable. The stranger must think she was some kind of lunatic, some weird Richard III fan-girl, but *tough*! Not his business. As long as he wasn't out to grab her bag or grab her, she didn't much care what he thought.

She tried to focus on the man again; he stood before the statue of Richard III, staring up at it through the welter of the rain, as if he could not quite believe what he was seeing. He couldn't be a local then, if he seemed so surprised; the statue had stood there since the 1980's, a gift of the Richard III Society. Through her hazy, water-blurred vision, she could catch fleeting glimpses of dark hair, wavy, its highlights slightly reddish in the headlamps of the passing cars. Lots of hair, unfashionably long, and a short, pale, serious face with a determined chin and a mouth thin but not cruel. A face unexpectedly youthful, even attractive.

There was a sudden shock of familiarity...and the reason was too ridiculous, too unbelievable to contemplate; her mind could not accept it. If it did, surely she would faint, go mad, or drop dead on the spot...

"*He was a good king, really...Richard,*" she squeaked and she did not know if she used the King's name to refer to the maligned ruler dead over 500 years...or to the man who stood at the base of the King's statue, so close she could reach out and touch him, if she dared. But she would never dare; what if he vanished like smoke or fell to dust before her eyes? Her cheeks drained to ashen-grey—then she turned and fled out of Castle Park onto the street, into the bright lights and relative normality of Leicester's city centre.

In the park, Richard continued to stand at the foot of his own memorial statue, lashed by raindrops and skirling wind. He noted that the statue bore only a truncated dagger now, thanks to the depredations of vandals; but soon it would have a sword again, when what was broken would be mended anew.

Resurgam. He placed the sword-hilt of Truth is My Light on the plinth, his own tribute. *I shall rise again.*

Gazing into the rain on that stormy night near the Anniversary of Bosworth, the time of his death, the time of his rebirth over 500 years later, the King whispered with fervour:

"*Richard liveth yet.*"

THE END (?)

POSTSCRIPT

In March of 2015 they buried, not Richard Plantagenet, but his frail, battle-scarred bones. J

Just a few days after an eclipse of the sun; the same one, on its great cycle, that had heralded the tragic death of Anne Neville.

Near the obliterated site of Greyfriars, they placed his body in the cathedral that was once merely the parish church of St Martins, now elevated in status to utmost eminence.

Thousands had come to witness that moment of changed history, lining the streets of the ancient town; through the sky white roses rained to slide like tears over the smooth lid of the wooden coffin wrought by a descendant's hand.

Richard's remains had been carried in a hearse to Bosworth Field, where canons were fired and earth from Fenn Lane, Middleham and Fotheringhay gathered and placed reverently beside his wrapped bones. A rosary fashioned to semblance of his lady mother's also lay beside him, accompanying him through eternity. Amidst waiting crowds both young and old, he was carried at last back across Bow Bridge into Leicester…this time, more than five centuries later, in triumph not in shame.

Some had feared those who scorned or even felt unnatural hatred for a man long gone might react with protest or foolish gesture; they did not. The haters confined their blusterings to a voracious and capricious media; very often, they were scorned, excoriated for their rude disrespect, even laughed at.

The coffin was lowered into a brick-lined vault by soldiers, as was apt, for Richard was a soldier, England's last great warrior king; the great slab of Swaledale stone was then drawn over him.

The finders, their destinies forever now entwined with Richard's, bowed before the King in final salute. His funeral crown, now safely encased, gleamed brightly in the dim cathedral aisle for all to see.

The King lost, the king returned to his estate. The circle turned; the past had changed and a million old history books, with their nonsense about empty, anachronistic horse-trough coffins and vengeful mobs hurling bones into the river Soar, were slammed shut forever.

And the city of Leicester burned with fire on the final night of remembrance, a thousand or more candles alight on pavement and hanging in sparse, as yet unbudded trees, candles to burn away the shadows, candles that issued sweet scent like the incense of the churches of old.

Candles to light the path from darkness to eternal Light for the long dead King.

Caught in webs of flame and darkness, Richard was there, unseen, unnoticed amidst the crowds. Had anyone noticed him, he would have seemed just a man. Another spectator, perhaps a mourner. A young man with a face out of time.

But as the last of the night's fireworks shot high above the cathedral and its sparks fell in burning glory about the lofty spire, he raised his arms to the sky as if in supplication…and he was gone, flickering out like one of the many candles burning throughout Leicester, departing on his journey to seek the ultimate Truth, and to reunite with those he had loved and lost so long ago.

But although he had given up earthly form again, he knew his essence was still there, would always be, even when he obtained the ultimate mystery that he sought.

Whenever the living thought of him, he too would live.

There was still much to be done to clear his reputation, to unravel the mysteries of his time, his brief and tragic reign. Still many lies and ingrained myths to be dispersed, like the hunchback, the withered arm, the limp born of exaggeration and authorly imaginings.

He would be there, in some way, to see it done.

'And then I can never really die, can I?'

Excerpt from ASTROLABIUS by Ella Wheeler Wilcox

I wrenched from a passing comet in its flight,
By that great force of two mad hearts aflame,
A soul incarnate, back to earth you came,
To glow like star-dust for a little night.
Deep shadows hide you wholly from our sight;
The centuries leave nothing but your name,
Tinged with the lustre of a splendid shame,
That blazed oblivion with rebellious light.

The mighty passion that became your cause,
 Still burns its lengthening path across the years;
We feel its raptures, and we see its tears
And ponder on its retributive laws.
Time keeps that deathless story ever new;
Yet finds no answer, when we ask of you.

Author's Note. Aug 1 2014

Why Richard III? Why Fantasy?

When Richard III's remains were found at Greyfriars, like millions of others, I was captivated by the story of the dig. Nearly 30 years earlier I had read the marvelous Sunne in Splendour by Sharon Penman, and that led me to study Richard's life and times. However, in the intervening years, I had 'strayed' somewhat from the Middle Ages, into the realms of the prehistoric, my main area of expertise.

Joining various online groups after Richard was found, I was amazed to witness the passions that could still be roused for this long dead king, both 'pro' and 'ante.' Sometimes it felt like the Wars of the Roses were being fought all over again!

I began to think about the appeal Richard had to his modern supporters, beyond the restoration of his good name and righting an old injustice. There seemed, sometimes, to be an almost 'mystical' connection as evidenced in the book SECRET HISTORY by John Dening, where the author claims to have contacted the King through a medium. I wondered if archetypes were coming into play—something that speaks to humanity in general—a young, heroic and doomed man, who was also in this instance the 'scapegoat', another powerful symbolic figure in its own right.

So I decided to see if I could meld both history and fantasy together to bring forward these ancient archetypes in fiction, paying particular attention to the legend of the 'Sacred King' or Year King who is sacrificed to the Land in time of war or famine, while another takes his place. Evidence of these primitive kingship rituals may well be found in Iron Age bodies such as Lindow Man in England, and Old Croghan and Clonycavan man in Ireland. All of these burials seem to be high status men who suffered 'overkill' multiple wounds, which included head trauma, strangulation and mutilation, before being deposited naked in bogs, sometimes on land boundaries, probably to appease chthonic gods. Many of them had physical defects or an attribute that made them 'different' within their community—Lindow III had an extra thumb while Old Croghan man was 6ft 6, a virtual giant in his time. Although not male, so not a 'king,' a female bog body from the Netherlands who underwent similar sacrificial rites suffered scoliosis, as did King Richard. I could see echoes, undoubtedly coincidental but mythically strong, of this rite in the death of Richard, who was slain in the heart of England, in the marshy bogs on Redemore, suffering humiliation injuries as his naked body was taken away over a horse's back.

At first, my plan for the story was quite a simple fantasy one.... I was going to use the old legend of Thomas Rhymer and have the King taken into the otherworld after the battle by the Queen of Faerie, where he was called to do battle with the infamous Leicestershire witch, Black Annis, a child-eating hag rumoured to live in a cave in the Dane Hills. Then strange coincidences started happening. I discovered that the legend of True Thomas actually HAD a historical connection to Bosworth! Tudor had manipulated one of Thomas's prophecies to announce his victory at a place called 'Sandeford.' I then also discovered another prophet, Robert Newton, whose origins were more obscure; some said he lived in the 15th century, others several hundred years later. His prophecies were clearly based on Thomas the Rhymer's, but there were many additional ones that were much more relevant to Bosworth than Thomas's. I thought it incredibly haunting when one line of such a prophecy referred to 'finding the bones of a British king'—maybe there was something in those prophecies, after all!

Black Annis herself even ended up with a hitherto unknown connection to Richard III—I discovered the first ever reference to the witch was in a poem written by one of the Herrick (Heyrick) family. The Herricks were lucky enough to have a marvelous garden in Leicester...which also happened to be on the site of Greyfriars and contained the tomb of King Richard. Black Annis (or Agnes Black) is also sometimes said in local lore to be the old hag on Bow Bridge, who prophesied that Richard's head would hit the stonework upon his return from battle. This hag who predicts the demise of a hero at a fording place in a river is a mythic figure in herself—the Celtic *Bean-Nighe*, or Washer at the Ford. Such a creature also appears in the earliest versions of the Robin Hood legend, foretelling Robin's death.

As I wrote the story and added in all these mythic and folkloric elements, the story outline itself began to change and become much darker, almost a Dante's Inferno type quest for absolution rather than a simple 'quest' story as intended. Allegory was now mingled with the traditional fantasy elements.

All of the folksongs and poems used in SACRED KING are from authentic ancient sources, though I may have played with the words here and there, and edited them down : The Havamal, John Barleycorn, The Corpus Christi Carol, Lavender's Green, The Dream of the Rood. Newton's prophecies, as spoken by the Queen of Elfland, are authentic, but I have picked out the most relevant lines to the subject of King Richard and Bosworth Field.

All historical places in the story and the details given about them are real (other than in Elfland, of course!), and outside the fantasy scenario, the historical events are real. Obviously, they are my take on them and may have a bit of 'tweaking' here and there for dramatic effect and flow—we don't know, for instance, if Richard's friend Francis Lovell was at Bosworth or not. He may have still been on the road from the south coast. However, like many other authors, I have placed him on the battlefield with his long-time friend that fateful day. Also, some accounts say William Stanley placed Richard's crown on Tudor's head, others say Thomas (I went with the latter due to Thomas being Henry's step-father.) I have the left the 'mystery of the princes' as just that, a mystery… but have dropped a few hints here and there about potential 'suspects'.

And you may wonder, have I had any mystical experiences? Well, recently I was using a wonderful little gizmo on the net, a leyline checker. Apparently a leyline runs from Middleham castle in Yorkshire straight through my house in Wiltshire….
J.P.R

OTHER BOOKS BY J.P. REEDMAN

If you have enjoyed my story, please checkout my other works, available on Amazon:
Other works on RICHARD III:

COMING THIS NOVEMBER, 2015. 'I, RICHARD PLANTAGENET.' A major full length novel. Richard as you have never seen him, from HIS OWN first person perspective. Funny, tragic, loyal and driven, warrior and good lord, lover and faithful husband; not Shakespeare's sinner but not a bloodless saint, either. A real man captured in the web of destiny.

Also:

TALES OF THE WHITE BOAR 1. A collection of short stories about Richard III

LOYAULTE—TALES OF THE WHITE BOAR 2. A second collection of short stories about Richard III

SONS OF YORK—Richard III and his Brothers. Short story collection

GOLDEN SUNNES AND WHITE ROSES- 156 page Anthology containing the three short story collections mentioned above.

STONE LORD. A retelling of the Arthurian legend with a twist—it is set in the Bronze Age, the era of Stonehenge. Real archaeology mixed with fiction, in the style of Jean Auel and Bernard Cornwell.

MOON LORD. Stand-alone sequel to STONE LORD. A prehistoric Game of Thrones culminating in destruction at Stonehenge